A GIRL CALLED JUSTICE

THE GHOST IN THE GARDEN

D1464565

ELLY Griffiths

A GIRL CALLED JUSTICE

THE GHOST IN THE GARDEN

Quercus

QUERCUS CHILDREN'S BOOKS

First published in Great Britain in 2021 by Hodder & Stoughton Limited

1 3 5 7 9 10 8 6 4 2

A CIP catalogue record for this book
is available from the British Library.

ISBN 978 1 78654133 8

Printed and bound in Great Britain by
Clays Ltd, Elcograf S.p.A.

The paper and board used in this book
are made from wood from responsible sources.

Quercus Children's Books
An imprint of
Hachette Children's Group
Part of Hodder & Stoughton Limited
Carmelite House
50 Victoria Embankment
London EC4Y 0DZ

An Hachette UK Company
www.hachette.co.uk

www.hachettechildrens.co.uk

For JAM – Juliet, Alex and Monique

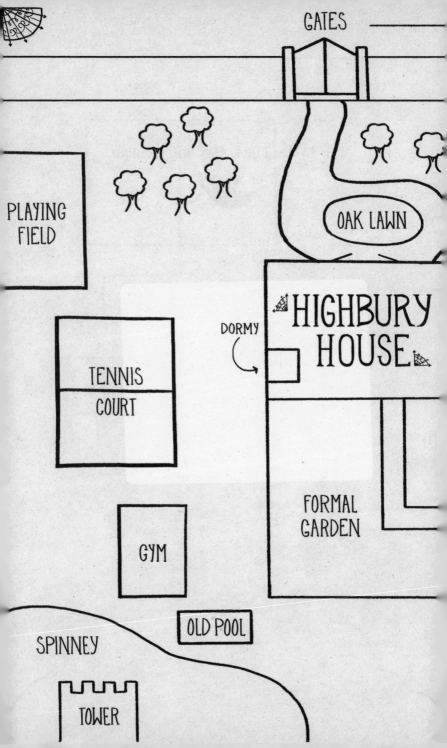

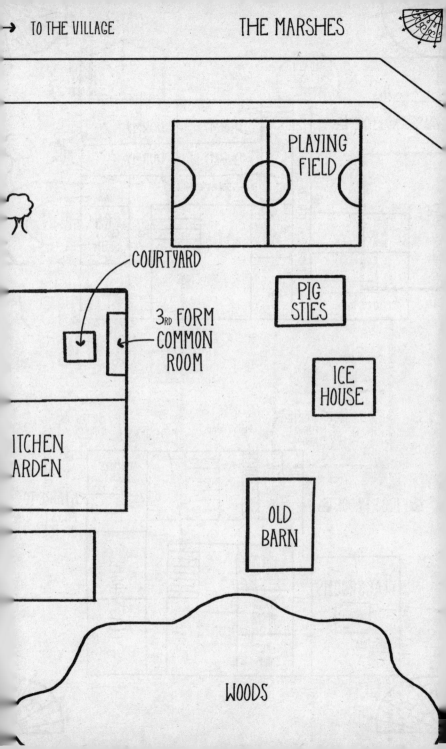

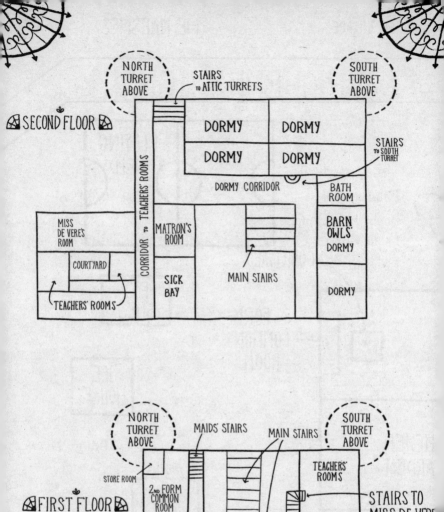

SECOND FLOOR

NORTH TURRET ABOVE

STAIRS to ATTIC TURRETS

SOUTH TURRET ABOVE

DORMY DORMY

DORMY DORMY

STAIRS to SOUTH TURRET

DORMY CORRIDOR

BATH ROOM

CORRIDOR to TEACHERS' ROOMS

MISS DE VERE'S ROOM

MATRON'S ROOM

BARN OWLS' DORMY

COURTYARD

MAIN STAIRS

SICK BAY

TEACHERS' ROOMS

DORMY

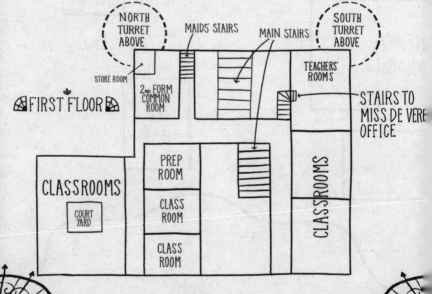

FIRST FLOOR

NORTH TURRET ABOVE

MAIDS' STAIRS

MAIN STAIRS

SOUTH TURRET ABOVE

STORE ROOM

2ND FORM COMMON ROOM

TEACHERS' ROOMS

STAIRS TO MISS DE VERE OFFICE

CLASSROOMS

PREP ROOM

COURT YARD

CLASS ROOM

CLASS ROOM

CLASSROOMS

◢ HIGHBURY HOUSE ◣

School for the Daughters of Gentlefolk

Staff

Headmistress	—	Miss Dolores de Vere
Deputy Headmistress and Latin Mistress	—	Miss Brenda Bathurst
Mathematics Mistress	—	Miss Edna Morris
English Mistress	—	Miss Susan Crane
History Mistress	—	Miss Ada Hunting
Science and Cookery Mistress	—	Miss Eloise Loomis
Drama and Elocution Mistress	—	Miss Joan Balfour
Music and Geography Mistress	—	Miss Myfanwy Evans
French Master	—	Monsieur Jean-Maurice Pierre
Games Mistress	—	Miss Margaret Heron
Matron	—	Miss Grace Macintosh
Housekeeper	—	Mrs Jean Hopkirk
Groundsman and Handyman	—	Mr Robert Hutchins

Form 3 at Highbury House

Form Mistress: Miss Hunting

Irene Atkins	Flora McDonald
Alicia Butterfield	Elizabeth Moore
Moira Campbell	Freda Saxon-Johnson
Cecilia Delaney	Leticia Smith
Eva Harris-Brown	Susan Smythe
Stella Goldman	Rose Trevellian-Hayes
Joan Kirby	Nora Wilkinson
Justice Jones	Letitia Blackstock

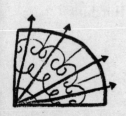

CHAPTER 1

September 1937

'It seems strange to think that we'll be third years,' said Stella.

'Yes,' said Justice. 'I thought I'd get expelled long before this.'

Stella laughed, but Justice wasn't entirely sure that she had been joking. She thought back to the first time she'd seen Highbury House, almost exactly a year ago. She had been on her own then, sitting in the back of a taxi, trying desperately not to show how scared she felt. She'd never been to boarding school before; she'd never been to any kind of school. She remembered how Highbury House had loomed up out of the darkness, its four turrets black against the sky, and she had thought: *This is the perfect place for a murder.*

Today was very different. They were being driven by Justice's father, Herbert Jones, and Justice was with her best friend, Stella. She'd never had a best friend before – except Peter, who was more like a brother – and now she had two: Stella and Dorothy. Nothing, not even going back to boarding school, seems as bad when you have a friend with you.

Stella lived near Justice in London so it was easy for Herbert to take them both back. Besides, Stella's father's ancient car had finally broken down for good. Justice knew that she should feel sorry about this but she was just happy to have Stella's company. Even though she knew the school now, it was still daunting to think that, in a few minutes, they would see the headmistress, Miss de Vere, and all the other teachers, not to mention their fellow pupils.

'There it is!' said Stella.

It was a bright September afternoon so the school didn't look quite as much like a haunted castle as usual. It was still ridiculously large and gloomy, rising up out of the flat marshland like some sort of mirage, but when you know every inch of a place it somehow loses its power to terrify you. Justice had even explored the attics and the cellars, although these were strictly out of bounds.

'Do try not to break so many rules this year, Justice,' said her father. It was as if he had read her mind.

'I only do that when I'm trying to solve a mystery,' protested Justice. But her father was laughing. He was a lawyer, so Justice supposed that he was used to people breaking rules.

'There aren't going to be any mysteries this term,' said Stella. She sounded hopeful.

Justice knew that Stella didn't enjoy adventures as much as she did but she couldn't help hoping for a little excitement. Not an actual murder – just something unusual happening. Something a little out of the ordinary.

At that moment, a headless horseman reared up in front of them.

Justice screamed, although afterwards she wished she hadn't. Herbert swore and slammed on the brakes.

'The headless horseman,' breathed Stella. Their friend, Nora, had told them this ghost story last term.

'Nonsense,' said Herbert. 'It's a girl in a hood.'

Justice wound down her window and saw that Dad was right. It was a girl in a black cloak on a white horse. The horse was beautiful, with a flowing mane and tail, but it seemed agitated, half rearing, its nostrils wide.

'What were you playing at?' the girl shouted at Dad. 'Road hog!'

Dad didn't reply that the girl had just appeared from

nowhere. He got out of the car. 'Are you all right?' He extended a hand towards the frightened horse.

'Don't touch Cloud!'

Justice opened the car door. But, before she could move any further, two other horses suddenly emerged from a gap in the hedge, further up the road. They were ridden by adults in proper riding clothes: breeches, boots and tweed hacking jackets.

'Oh my goodness, Letitia,' said the woman, riding a brown horse. 'What happened?'

'This man nearly killed me,' said the girl. Letitia.

'You crossed the road without looking,' said Dad, but mildly.

'You can't go galloping off like that, Letitia,' said the man, who was riding a huge black horse. 'You could have been killed.' He raised his hat to Dad. 'Thank you for stopping so quickly, Mr Jones.'

And, with that, he turned and clattered away up the road. The two other horses followed him. Justice watched as they found the gap in the hedge and cantered off over the field, black, white and brown manes flying.

Herbert got back into the car and grinned at the two girls.

'Well, that was an adventure.'

They agreed that it was. But Justice was thinking: how had the man known Dad's name?

4

CHAPTER 2

After this excitement, the journey passed in a flash. In a few minutes they were driving through the stone gates with the griffins on top, past the sign saying, 'Highbury House Boarding School for the Daughters of Gentlefolk' and along the long driveway that led to the main entrance. Herbert parked by the huge oak doors and, as if from nowhere, Hutchins the handyman appeared to take Justice's and Stella's trunks.

Justice had been wondering if they'd meet the new matron, Miss Macintosh, but, to her surprise, it was Miss de Vere herself who floated down the steps to greet them.

'It's good to see you, Herbert.'

'Good to see you too, Dolores.'

The adults shook hands and Stella pulled Justice to one side.

'Did your dad just call Miss de Vere *Dolores*?'

'Yes,' said Justice. 'They're old friends.' As a matter of fact, Justice didn't like it when her father talked to her headmistress, though she couldn't quite have said why. Partly it was because she didn't want her home life and her school life overlapping. She wanted to be able to tell Dad how awful the teachers were and how inedible the school meals. She didn't want Miss de Vere putting her oar in and probably complaining about Justice's behaviour. But, most of all, Justice's mother had only been dead for a year. Justice never wanted her father to look at another woman, much less be smiling at her as he was doing now.

'How are you, Justice?' Miss de Vere turned to her. 'Did you have a good summer holiday?'

'Yes,' said Justice. Adding, 'Miss de Vere', after a look from Dad.

'And you, Stella? How are you and all your family? I'm looking forward to welcoming your sister Sarah here next year.'

'They're all OK,' said Stella, standing on one leg as she always did when she felt awkward. 'Sarah's looking forward to coming.'

'That's good,' said Miss de Vere. 'Herbert, could I have a word before you go?' And she drifted away to welcome some other parents.

'Bye, Justice.' Dad kissed her. 'Have a good term. Don't forget to write.'

'Bye, Dad.' As always, when it was time to say goodbye, Justice felt her chest constrict. School wasn't too bad but it was hard not to be able to see Dad for weeks, not until the first half holiday. Before she could say anything else, though, there was a thunderous sound of horses' hooves. Letting go of Dad, Justice saw three familiar riders cantering up the sweeping driveway.

The white horse came to a halt beside Dad's car. The girl swung down in one easy movement and thrust her reins into the woman's hands.

'Bye, Ma. Bye, Pa.' She didn't even turn to look at her parents.

Miss de Vere came hurrying over. Was she about to tell the new girl that horses weren't allowed at Highbury House? It seemed not. 'Welcome, dear Letitia,' said the headmistress. 'I'm sure you'll be very happy here. Now, who can I find to look after you?'

Don't look at me, prayed Justice. *Look over there. Rose has just arrived. She'd simply love to be friends with dear Letitia.*

'Justice Jones,' said Miss de Vere. 'Will you take Letitia under your wing?'

Justice and Stella showed Letitia the way to the dormitories, through the great hall, up the main staircase, along the corridor lined with suits of armour and gloomy old paintings, through the double doors, along another corridor, up some stone steps, down some more, past the door that led to the sick bay . . .

'How big is this place?' said Letitia. 'It didn't look that big from the outside, but we've been walking for miles.'

'It's not as big as it seems,' said Justice. 'It's just they make it very difficult to go from one place to another.'

'Because the most direct route is usually out of bounds,' said Stella.

'Do you know which dormy you're in?' said Justice, pushing open the door to the dormitory corridor. The familiar scent of damp and floor polish came up to greet her.

'It's on my letter,' said Letitia, taking a piece of paper out of her pocket. She was still wearing riding breeches, boots, a black jumper and the cloak. 'Yes, here it is. I'm in Barnowls.'

Stella and Justice looked at each other.

'We're in Barnowls but . . .'

Justice was about to say that they already had five people

8

in their dormy but Letitia had seen the name on a nearby door and pushed it open.

Justice and Stella followed her.

They saw immediately that another bed had been added. Nora and Eva, their classmates, were already there, chatting as they put away their outdoor clothes.

'Justice! Stella!' Nora came over to hug them. She was a tall girl with glasses that were always slightly askew. She was the form storyteller and impressionist. Justice hugged Nora back, realising how much she'd missed her over the holidays.

Eva, a small girl with wispy blonde hair, came bounding over too.

'It's simply super to see you—' She stopped, catching sight of Letitia, standing in the doorway in her black cloak.

'This is Letitia,' said Justice. 'She's in Barnowls too.'

'Super,' said Eva faintly.

Another voice sounded from the doorway: 'Hallo, chaps. What's this? Someone's put another bed here by mistake.'

'Rose,' said Justice. 'This is Letitia. She's a new girl.'

Rose turned her icy blue gaze on Letitia.

'It must be a mistake,' she said. 'There are always five people in this dormy. There isn't room for more.'

It was true that the sixth bed did make the small room very crowded.

'No mistake,' said Letitia cheerfully. 'It says here that I'm in Barnowls. Bagsy the bed by the window.'

'You can't bagsy a bed,' said Rose in outrage. 'You're new. You have last choice. I'm the dormy captain. I get the bed by the window.'

'I was here first,' said Letitia, throwing her overnight bag on to the bed. 'The bed's mine.'

'I'm the dormy captain,' said Rose, stamping her foot.

'You must tell me why that's important one day,' said Letitia.

Justice and Stella exchanged another glance. Justice wasn't sure if she liked the new girl but she was certainly going to make the autumn term a lot more interesting.

CHAPTER 3

It was a subdued set of Barnowls who trooped downstairs to Meal. Letitia was now wearing school uniform – brown blazer, brown skirt, yellow and white striped shirt, brown socks – but she still didn't seem like the others.

Somehow the clothes looked slightly different on Letitia; maybe because she'd tied her curly brown hair back with a bootlace. But it was also partly because she seemed so unconcerned, walking along, head high, humming quietly under her breath. Justice remembered this time last year, when Eva had led her to the dining room for the first time. She had tried to be brave (she remembered repeating an old saying of Mum's to herself: 'Screw your courage to the sticking place') but, deep down, she'd been terrified. Justice had never been to boarding school before and had had no idea what to expect. From a casual remark dropped by Letitia earlier it seemed that this was the same with her: she'd previously been taught by a governess at home. So this huge, echoing house, girls streaming down the stairs, all looking identical in their brown; the dining room with its hubbub of scraping chairs and clattering cutlery – it would all be totally new to Letitia.

You wouldn't have known it, though. Letitia pushed in front of Rose; said, 'No thanks, it looks ghastly' when offered a helping of the junket known to the girls as dead baby; took two slices of bread, and looked round for somewhere to sit.

'The Barnowl table is over there,' said Eva helpfully.

'Do you mean I've got to sit with you lot for every meal?'

'Er . . . yes.' Eva looked around rather desperately at the others.

'Why don't you go and sit with the prefects instead?' said Rose. 'I'm sure they'd simply love to have you.'

Justice looked over to the prefects' table and her heart sank. What was Helena Bliss doing there? The head girl had been in the upper sixth last year and Justice had assumed that she would have now left school. But Helena was still there, her golden hair loose on her shoulders, looking haughtily around the room. She caught Justice looking at her and raised her eyebrows slightly.

'Rose!' hissed Justice. 'Why is Helena still here?' Rose always seemed to know about Helena probably because she was, by her own admission, a mini version of the head girl.

'She's decided to stay on for an extra term,' said Rose. 'Before she goes on to finishing school in Switzerland.'

'I heard she'd failed her matric,' said Nora.

This seemed much more likely. Helena was excellent at looking superior, but Justice had often wondered how much interest she really took in lessons. When Helena had played Alice in *Alice in Wonderland* in the school play last year, she'd spent most of the time adjusting her hairband.

'Helena wouldn't *fail*,' said Rose, putting a tiny amount of dead baby on her plate.

'She's the cleverest person in the *world*,' said Eva, overdoing it as usual.

Letitia had obviously decided to sit with them after all. She had plonked herself down at the table and was now spreading butter on her bread. She was about to take a bite when Eva put an anxious hand on her arm.

'We can't eat until Helena says Grace.'

'I'm not waiting,' said Letitia. 'I'm hungry.' And she took a big mouthful of bread. The Barnowls stared, obviously expecting the sky to fall in and demons to appear to drag the new girl straight to hell. But all that happened was that

Helena stood up and said, '*Benedictus benedicat*,' and the girls fell on their revolting food with apparent relish.

'What are you looking forward to most about Highbury House, Letitia?' said Eva, with a kind of desperate friendliness. Justice admired her perseverance.

'Nothing,' said Letitia. She finished her bread and took an unenthusiastic sip of milk.

'Do you like games?' said Rose. She had been sports captain last year and was the star of the lacrosse team. Justice hated all sport, with the single exception of cross-country running.

'Never played any.' Letitia shrugged. 'I like horse riding, though.'

'How super,' said Eva. 'Have you got your own horse?'

'Yes. He's a grey called Cloud.' Letitia paused before adding, 'I'm going to miss him.'

'He's gorgeous,' said Justice. 'Stella and I saw Letitia riding him on the way here,' she told the other Barnowls.

'Yes, your father nearly ran us over,' said Letitia.

'You rode out in front of him,' Justice flared up.

She hadn't realised that she'd spoken loudly but Helena rose from the prefects' table and strode over. The Barnowls fell silent.

'Is that squabbling I hear?' said Helena. 'We can't have that. Little birds in their nests agree. Remember that, girls.'

'Yes, Helena.'

'Sorry, Helena.'

'And I see we have a new girl.' Helena turned to Letitia. 'What's your name?'

'Letitia Blackstock. What's yours?'

Justice could hear audible gasps from the other girls. She was even quite shocked herself, which proved that Highbury House was starting to get to her.

'In this school,' said Helena grimly, 'we don't ask impertinent questions. It seems that you need taking down a peg or two.' And she turned on her heel and stalked away.

Letitia's shoulders were shaking.

'Don't worry.' Eva patted her shoulder. 'You weren't to know. You're new.'

But Letitia wasn't crying. She was laughing.

Justice had been hoping to see her other great friend, Dorothy. But Dorothy was a maid, which meant she was probably busy elsewhere. Plus, pupils weren't allowed to talk to the maids. Not that Justice took much notice of this rule, but it made proper conversation difficult. She usually resorted to visiting Dorothy's attic room in the middle of the night.

After Meal, they went to the common room. They had a new one now they were third years, on the ground floor, on one side of the courtyard. Justice didn't like it as much as the second-year common room, which had been on the first floor and away from the prying eyes of the teachers. This one was bigger though, and had a ping-pong table and an old wireless. The girls were thrilled with the wireless. Irene turned the dial until she found a music programme and then they were all were dancing madly around the room. Letitia, however, sat on her own reading a book called *How To School Your Pony*.

Should I talk to her? wondered Justice, breathless from waltzing with Stella. Miss de Vere had told her to take Letitia under her wing but Letitia didn't seem to need looking after and, besides, was likely to bite Justice's head off again. She was still trying to decide when the door opened and a voice said, 'Girls!'

They all stopped. In the background, Guy Lombardo continued to sing about September in the rain.

The figure in the doorway was wearing a nurse's uniform so it didn't take incredible detective skills to work out that this was the new matron. Justice had mixed feelings about the last two holders of this post so she observed the new school nurse with interest. She was younger than the other two, tall and slim with blonde hair in a bun and a composed, but not actually unfriendly, expression.

16

'Hallo, girls. Could someone turn off that noise? Mr Lombardo is all very well in his place but . . .'

A few girls laughed. Nora turned off the wireless.

'I'm Miss Macintosh, the new matron. A few of you haven't given in your health certificates.' She consulted a list. 'Stella Goldman, Justice Jones and Letitia Blackstock. Could you run upstairs and get them for me?'

Justice and Stella moved towards the door. Justice had been at Highbury House long enough to know that, when a member of staff asked you to do something, you did it immediately. But Letitia continued to read her book. The other third years – all fifteen of them – turned to stare at her.

'Letitia?' said Matron.

'I haven't got it,' said Letitia. 'My father said it would be all right.'

Fifteen girls held their breath. Thirty eyes swivelled to look at Matron.

Miss Macintosh seemed about to speak but then appeared to change her mind. She turned and left the room without another word.

The first night of a new term was usually rather fun. The Barnowls brought food from home and they ate it in the dormitory after lights out. It was very cosy, even if you were missing home, to sit on the floor wrapped in a blanket eating fruit cake. Nora usually told ghost stories and Eva invariably had an attack of the hiccoughs.

But Letitia's arrival changed everything. Justice offered her some cake but Letitia refused it and sat in her bed by the window reading her pony book by the light of a torch. Nora tried to tell her favourite ghost story but, somehow, it was hard to lose yourself in the tale of Grace Highbury (whose ghost was meant to haunt the Tower in the grounds) with a supercilious stranger sitting a few yards away. So, after eating their cake, the Barnowls climbed meekly into bed.

Justice wrote in her journal.

Day 1.
Everything is the same and yet it isn't. There's a new girl and I ought to like her – she's never been to boarding school before, thinks HH is a bit potty etc – but somehow I don't. There's some mystery about the way the new matron treated her too. Must discuss this with Dorothy tomorrow.

Plus: Helena Bliss is STILL here. At this rate she'll still be in the 6th when she's 100.

Number of times Eva has said 'super': 24

CHAPTER 4

After breakfast (grey, quivering porridge and burnt toast), the girls filed into the great hall for Miss de Vere's 'Welcome Back' assembly. Everyone always got very excited about this but, as far as Justice could remember, it was just a chance for the headmistress to give them a lecture on good behaviour and an excuse to sing the school song. Miss de Vere also announced the school captains, which was another cause of fevered speculation.

'I bet you'll be third-year form captain, Rose,' said her best friend, Alicia.

'It'll be hard to do that and be sports captain,' said Rose, flicking her blonde plaits. 'But I'm sure I'll manage.'

'Maybe you'll be form captain again,' whispered Justice to Stella. 'And sucks to Rose.'

'It's always a different captain every term,' said Stella. 'I think it'll be Alicia. Miss Hunting likes her.'

Their form mistress this year was Miss Hunting, who taught history. Justice liked history but she didn't think she was one of the teacher's favourites. She'd got extra prep last term for not paying attention in class.

The teachers were sitting in a line on the stage: Miss Heron, the games mistress, in her divided skirts; Miss Morris, the maths teacher; Miss Crane, who taught English; Monsieur Pierre, the French master; Miss Bathurst, the Latin mistress. And a new face: a face with a neat, black beard.

'It's a *man*,' hissed Eva.

'You don't say,' muttered Justice. By now, all the girls had realised that there was a new teacher and that he was – shock, horror – male. A whisper ran through the hall, gaining in strength and only stopping when Miss Evans, the music mistress, struck a chord on the piano and the cacophony began.

'Oh, Highbury,

From land to sea,

Our home in heart and mind.

However far our steps may roam,

They'll bring us back to thee . . .'

It was a truly terrible song but the girls sang it with

fervour. On Justice's left, Eva's eyes were shut and she looked as if she might be about to cry. *You and me both*, thought Justice. When would it end? There seemed to be about a million verses and Justice had never bothered to learn all the words. Looking past Eva, Justice caught Letitia's eye. The new girl winked at her.

When the last discordant notes died away, Miss de Vere made her way on to the platform. 'Please be seated, girls.'

Miss de Vere was a tall, elegant figure. The girls were always going on about how beautiful she was but the headmistress's eyes – though fine and dark – were too sharp for Justice's liking. She always looked as if she knew exactly what you were thinking.

'Welcome back to Highbury House and to the autumn term, when we prepare for the wonderful season of Christmas.' Miss de Vere embarked on one of her stories about animals storing up food for the winter. There must be a moral – there always was – but Justice wasn't sure what it was. Always make sure you have a store of nuts in case Cook's meals get even worse? Hide things in old tree trunks? She looked at Eva, who had her mouth open, and Rose, who was examining the ends of her hair. Once again she caught Letitia's eye and, once again, Letitia winked.

The story ended with the field mouse sharing its nuts

with other, less organised animals. Miss de Vere beamed around at the school. 'Now, a few announcements.'

Were they going to hear about the mysterious man? They were.

'We are pleased to welcome a new member of staff,' said Miss de Vere. 'Mr Davenport has joined us to teach art.' An excited murmur. They'd never had a proper art teacher before. Miss de Vere then informed them that the end of term play would be a pantomime. 'A good traditional form of entertainment.'

Justice silently betted that, if it was *Cinderella*, Helena would be the heroine and Justice would get the part of an ugly sister.

'And now for the form captains,' said Miss de Vere. Justice drifted away again. She thought of her mum's novel, *Murder in the Mansion*, when a man was killed whilst making a speech. A chandelier had dropped on his head, as Justice remembered. She looked up. No chandelier here, just a row of dusty bulbs. She supposed that even Hutchins couldn't reach up there to dust.

A nudge in the ribs brought her back to earth. 'It's our form,' said Stella.

'Third-year form captain,' Miss de Vere was saying, 'Justice Jones.'

Stella squeezed her hand. 'Well done!'

Justice felt quite stunned. She glanced at Rose and saw that she was feeling the same way. Eva and Nora were grinning, though. Letitia was scowling again. No wink this time.

'Third-year sports captain, Stella Goldman.'

Justice was straightforwardly delighted by this news. 'Congrats!' she whispered to Stella. She could sense Rose's annoyance from six feet away. Miss de Vere ended by saying that they were lucky to have their head girl, Helena Bliss, with them for another term. Everyone clapped. Except Justice and Letitia.

'School dismissed,' said Miss de Vere, as Miss Evans launched into another approximation of a tune. Justice thought it was 'To Be A Pilgrim', but she wasn't sure.

'Now that you're form captain,' said Miss Hunting, 'I expect to see a more responsible attitude from you, Justice.'

Justice knew by now that you had to answer teachers even when they hadn't asked a question.

'Yes, Miss Hunting.'

'And, now, let's turn our attention to the Tudors . . .'

Justice was glad that they had got to the Tudors after what seemed like years studying the Wars of the Roses.

23

Henry VIII and his six wives should be interesting anyway. It was while Miss Hunting was talking about the persecution of Catholics in Elizabeth's reign that Justice suddenly remembered something. She put up her hand.

'Yes, Justice?' There was a faint suggestion of 'Don't interrupt' in the teacher's voice.

'Miss Hunting, last year you said that there might be a priest's hole in Highbury House. A place where a Catholic priest might hide.'

'That's correct, Justice. I do believe that there's a priest's hole here. It might be the origin of one of the tunnels under the house. The whole area is dangerously unstable. And there's no money to make the necessary repairs. That is why it is expressly forbidden to enter the cellars without permission.' This time, she definitely gave Justice a warning look.

At the end of the class, Justice found herself next to Letitia. To her surprise, the new girl linked her arm with hers. 'I'd love to find a secret tunnel, wouldn't you?'

'I did find one last year,' Justice couldn't help saying. 'With my friend, Dorothy.'

'I knew it! Let's go exploring one day, you and I.'

'The cellar's out of bounds.' Justice wasn't sure what to make of this new, friendly Letitia. She'd often wished that

24

Stella was less scared of breaking school rules but, if she did any exploring, it would be with Stella or Dorothy, not Letitia.

'You don't care about that,' said Letitia. 'Nor do I. I thought we could be friends when I saw your face when all the little creeps were singing that horrible song. Then, when you were made form captain, I thought that maybe you were a creep too. But now I know you're not. Let's be friends, shall we?'

'Of course,' said Justice. Friends were always welcome, especially at boarding school, and Letitia certainly seemed as if she might be good fun. But, despite her many grumbles about her classmates, Justice didn't like them being called creeps. She was wondering how to say this – without sounding creepish herself – when Letitia propelled her forwards along the corridor, almost running.

As they passed Stella, Justice tried a helpless grin. It wasn't returned.

CHAPTER 5

The next lesson was ART, written in block capitals in Justice's new timetable. After lunch she had LATIN followed by DOUBLE GAMES. Letitia held on to Justice's arm as they climbed the three flights of stairs to the art room.

'I wonder what the new teacher will be like?' she said.

'Me too,' said Justice. 'We've never had proper art lessons before – just drawing flowers in botany.'

'Art should be a chance to have some fun,' said Letitia. 'Play a few tricks. That sort of thing.'

Justice was all for fun, in theory, but she couldn't help wondering exactly what Letitia meant. She looked around for Stella but she was several steps below, walking with Irene. Justice pushed open the double doors of what was known as 'the studio'. She'd spent a lot of time in this room last year, painting scenery for *Alice*, and always liked it. It was in the attic and had high ceilings, panelled walls and large windows that rattled when it was windy.

The girls burst in so noisily that it was a few minutes before they realised that Mr Davenport was already there. He was sitting behind an easel, frowning at the picture in front of him, not seeming to notice that sixteen schoolgirls had galumphed into the room. Gradually, the girls fell silent and sat on the chairs arranged in three rows. The art master had still not said a word.

'Do you think he's deaf?' Eva whispered to Nora.

'He's not deaf,' said a soft voice. 'But he is becoming rather bored.'

The girls exchanged glances. 'You and me both,' muttered Letitia to Justice. She had somehow inserted herself in the seat Justice had saved for Stella.

'Stand up,' said Mr Davenport, remaining seated himself. The girls looked at each other. 'Stand up,' said the teacher again, still in the same quiet tone. The girls stood.

'We're going outside,' said Mr Davenport. 'Leave your bags here but pick up a sketchbook by the door. I'll meet you by the oak tree on the front lawn.' Nobody moved. 'Go on!' Mr Davenport's voice was low, with a hint of an accent. Justice

28

couldn't quite place it but she was sure that Nora would be able to impersonate the new teacher by the end of the day.

The girls clattered back down the three flights of stairs and out through the main doors. This time Justice managed to position herself next to Stella.

'Why are we going outside?' said Stella.

'I don't know,' said Justice. Usually they only went into the grounds for games, or walks on Wednesday afternoons. Lessons at Highbury House were mostly spent copying things off the blackboard and reading from textbooks. Some teachers, like Miss Hunting, allowed brief discussions, but mostly the girls had to sit at their desks in silence. Justice didn't think that any of the teachers would ever suggest going *outdoors* to learn.

The front lawn was a smooth circle, mown every day. In the centre was a magnificent tree with spreading branches. Justice assumed this was the oak. The girls stood in its shade and waited in silence until Mr Davenport joined them.

'What are you waiting for?' asked the art teacher. 'Draw!'

'Draw what?' said someone.

'Draw the tree,' said Mr Davenport. 'Or the house or the flowers or the pig bins. Just draw what's in front of your eyes. Lie on the grass if you want and draw the shapes of the leaves against the sky. See the beauty in nature.'

'What if the grass is wet?' asked Rose.

'Then you'll get wet,' said Mr Davenport.

It was actually a beautiful autumn day, warm with a slight breeze rippling through the wheat in the fields behind the house. Feeling very daring, Justice lay on her back beneath the branches of the oak tree, and looked up. The sky was very blue and the leaves looked almost translucent, their edges curly and distinct. Justice started to draw them but she kept getting little black dots in front of her eyes. She was aware of someone lying next to her and thought it was Stella but, when she turned her head, it was Letitia.

'This is a lark,' said Letitia. 'I'm going to draw a pig flying overhead.'

Justice sat up. Stella was standing a few feet away, drawing the house. Eva, who liked art, was lying on the grass too, sketching vigorously. Rose screamed that a snail had bitten her. Nora dropped her glasses. Mr Davenport sat propped against the tree trunk with his eyes closed.

'My tree doesn't look like a tree,' said Alicia.

'Art is about experimenting with reality,' said Mr Davenport, without opening his eyes.

'What if we see a ghost?' said Nora. 'Shall we draw that?'

'Of course,' said Mr Davenport. 'Only a fool would dismiss the existence of ghosts.'

Justice didn't believe in ghosts. In her experience, the living were more frightening than the dead. Did that make her a fool? She didn't think it was worth saying this, though, and concentrated on her artwork. It was very frustrating. She knew what she wanted to draw but didn't seem able to make her pencil do what she wanted.

After about twenty minutes, Mr Davenport stood up and said, 'Inside.' Then he strode off without bothering to see if they were following him.

Back in the studio, Mr Davenport collected their sketchbooks and looked at them in silence.

'Whose is this?' he said at last. He held up a drawing of the house, very big and bold, taking up all the page.

'Please, miss. It's mine,' said Eva.

The girls started to giggle.

'You don't have to call me "miss",' said Mr Davenport. 'I think "sir" is what's expected here. What's your name?'

'Eva, miss. Sir.'

'You've got a talent, Eva,' said Mr Davenport. 'I shall enjoy teaching you.'

He looked through the other books without comment. Then he handed them back. To Justice, he said, 'Promising, but let yourself go a bit. Don't be too precise.' To Letitia, 'That pig is out of proportion. It's almost bigger than the house.' Then, to the class in general, 'Keep your sketchbooks and draw in them as often as you can. Draw faces, fruit, eyes and hands. Draw anything that's an interesting shape or texture. Draw beautiful things and ugly things. Class dismissed.'

And he went back to his easel. Justice stole a look as she went past. It looked as if the teacher had started drawing Irene but had been distracted by the panelled wall behind him. Certainly there was more detail in the background than in Irene's face, which was a strange blur dominated by her glasses.

Justice managed to sit next to Stella at lunch, which was as disgusting as ever. Stella seemed a bit quiet but she cheered up when Nora started impersonating Mr Davenport. Justice looked around the dining hall for Dorothy, who sometimes helped clearing away the plates, but there was no sign of her friend. Justice felt that she needed Dorothy's opinion on Letitia, Mr Davenport and, well, everything really.

Latin was rather boring after the excitement of the morning. They had to translate a passage in their primer and Justice felt her attention drifting. When she shut her eyes she could still see the shape of the oak leaves.

After recess, the girls trooped out again for games.

Miss Heron met them at the gymnasium but, to Justice's

disappointment, told them to get changed and bring their lacrosse sticks. Even with a sympathetic teacher, Justice still couldn't get the hang of the game. She could never catch the ball in the net and keep it in there – 'cradling', it was called – and, after a bit, the girls stopped passing to her. Justice trotted around the outside of the pitch, thinking about Dad working away in his chambers, about her friend Peter at music school, about autumn walks in Hyde Park with Mum and collecting conkers and fallen leaves, going home to cocoa and crumpets . . .

'Justice!'

The ball was coming towards her. Justice took an almighty swing at it, missed and fell on her face. Someone laughed. She heard Miss Heron asking if she was all right.

'Fine, thanks.' Justice scrambled to her feet, trying to look as if she'd meant to take a flying dive into the mud.

'Cheer up,' said Miss Heron. 'Cross-country training will start soon.'

'Can't wait,' said Justice. At the other end of the pitch, Rose scored again.

As the girls showered and changed, Justice heard some of them complimenting Letitia: 'You're a natural.' 'I can't believe you haven't played before.'

'It's not difficult,' said Letitia, shrugging.

'Justice finds it difficult,' said Rose. 'Don't you?'

'Very difficult,' said Justice. *Always answer a hostile question briefly and truthfully*. That's what Dad always said.

All the same, Justice didn't want to walk with the others while they talked about how well Rose and Letitia had played. She took the long way back to the house and Stella loyally kept her company. The Tower stood on its own, surrounded by trees. Although she didn't believe it was haunted, Justice had had some nasty experiences in the sinister building. They gave it a wide berth now and, as they passed the spinney, they saw Miss Morris, the maths teacher, walking her Alsatian dog, Sabre. Sabre looked at Justice and wagged his tail – they were old friends – but he was too well-trained to bark or come over. Justice and Stella took the path that led to the walled kitchen gardens and, as they got closer, they heard a familiar voice.

'That's Helena Bliss,' said Justice.

Helena was standing by the gate talking to someone they couldn't see.

'Why isn't she in uniform?' said Stella.

Helena was wearing a flowery dress and straw hat. She was talking and laughing so animatedly that she didn't see them go past. Justice looked back to see who Helena was talking to and got a glimpse of a man digging in the vegetable beds. Justice couldn't see his face but he was youngish, with light brown hair.

'Is that a new gardener?' Justice asked Stella.

'I suppose so. I haven't seen him before.'

Helena's laugh rang out again across the grounds.

'Here we go again,' said Justice.

CHAPTER 6

After Meal, Justice saw Dorothy for the first time. She was carrying a tray of dirty crockery so Justice couldn't hug her, but they stood and grinned at each other in the little passage that led from the scullery to the kitchens.

'Where have you been?' asked Justice. 'I've been looking for you everywhere.'

'Working,' said Dorothy, with a grin. 'Cleaning, dusting, washing up . . .'

Justice felt slightly rebuked. She often almost forgot that Dorothy wasn't another pupil, that her job at Highbury House was to clean up after Justice and her friends. In the summer holidays, Dorothy had come to stay with Justice in London and there they'd been friends and equals, going boating on the Serpentine, watching a West End show, listening to the wireless in the evenings. But now, at school, Dorothy was about to wash dirty dishes and Justice was on her way to prep.

'Shall I come to see you tonight?' said Justice. 'Then you can tell me all your news. All about your family.' Dorothy had three sisters and two brothers. Justice, an only child, loved to hear stories about them.

'There's not much news,' said Dorothy. 'Tommy's walking now and John's left school.' Tommy was the baby and John was thirteen, Justice's age.

'Maybe I could come to the cottage again,' said Justice. 'Miss de Vere let me before.'

'I hope so!' Dorothy's face lit up. 'And, yes, come to my room tonight. Come at midnight.'

'You always say midnight,' laughed Justice. 'It's too hard to stay awake. I'll come at ten thirty, or as soon as everyone's asleep.'

Dorothy looked as if she was about to argue (she loved midnight meetings), but Cook started to shout for her and so she just said, 'See you then!' and scuttled off into the kitchen.

The Barnowls seemed to take an infuriatingly long time to get to sleep. First Eva and Nora were whispering then, when Rose told them to be quiet, Letitia started doing fake snores which made Eva laugh and, eventually, gave her hiccoughs.

Finally, though, Eva's hiccoughs turned to the squeaks she always made when she slept. In the bed next to Justice, Stella was breathing deeply and steadily. Justice looked at her watch, which she'd kept under her pillow alongside her torch. Ten o'clock. She'd wait until half past and then she'd go to the attics to see Dorothy.

Justice usually found that reciting murder trials kept her awake.

Rex v Stanley
Rex v Donagh and West
Rex v Hamilton
Rex v Pewsey

The trouble was that Justice was tired after her first day back. Her arm hurt from falling over during lacrosse and all her limbs felt as heavy as lead. When she closed her eyes it was if she was falling into a deep well of sleep. She had to keep them open.

Rex v Williams
Rex v Hughes
Rex v Bayliss and Bayliss
Rex v Peruzzi

She heard a snore, opened her eyes and realised that she had been the one snoring. She checked her watch. Twenty past ten. She had to go now or she'd fall asleep for good.

Justice got up quietly and, with the ease of long practice, crossed the room without treading on any of the creaking boards. She opened the door very slowly. Rose muttered crossly in her sleep but didn't wake as Justice slid out into the passage. Here too she had to avoid rickety floorboards, but Justice knew the way by now. She paused at the green baize door by Matron's room (the last two occupants had been rather too fond of sneaking around at night), but everything was silent. Justice pushed open the door.

'What are you doing?'

The voice was quiet but Justice jumped what felt like a mile into the air. She swung round to see Letitia grinning at her.

'Why are you following me?' Justice hissed.

'I wanted to see where you were going. There must be some mystery, otherwise you wouldn't have waited until everyone was asleep.'

'There's no mystery,' said Justice. 'I'm just going to see Dorothy, one of the maids. She's my friend and it's hard to chat during the day.'

'Great,' said Letitia. 'I'll come with you.'

'No,' said Justice, appalled.

'Yes.' Letitia was still grinning, her teeth gleaming in the darkness.

'You don't know Dorothy,' said Justice, rather desperately. It struck her as very foolish to be having a quarrel just a few feet from Matron's quarters.

'Well, now's my chance to get to know her,' said Letitia.

Justice turned her back and set off. She hoped that Letitia, despite her bold words, might not be brave enough to follow her but, as she crossed the landing and climbed the steps to the attic, she could hear the other girl just behind her.

Dorothy opened the door as soon as she heard footsteps.

'Justice! You're early. Oh . . .' She stared at Letitia.

'This is Letitia,' said Justice. 'I didn't want her to come. She just followed me.' She was fed up with trying to be nice.

'Hallo,' said Letitia. 'You must be Dorothy. Can we come in?'

Dorothy stood aside to let them in. Letitia looked round the attic room with frank curiosity. Justice was used to it by now. Dorothy's bed with its patchwork quilt looked almost cosy. She didn't see the bare floors or the high, uncurtained window. She didn't really even notice the bitter cold.

'Do you really sleep here?' said Letitia. 'It's horrible.'

'It's not too bad,' said Dorothy, sounding hurt. 'And I've got the place to myself.'

'It's a bit creepy,' said Letitia. 'But it would be a great place to hide. No one would think of looking here. Are there any other maids?'

'Ada comes from the village. There used to be another maid, Mary, but she . . .'

'What?' said Letitia.

'She died,' said Dorothy. She exchanged glances with Justice.

'What happened to her?' said Letitia.

'It's a long story,' said Justice.

'It was a mystery,' said Dorothy. 'And we solved it.'

Letitia sat on Dorothy's bed. 'Are there any mysteries this term?'

Justice felt extremely irritated. Mysteries were her thing, hers and Dorothy's. And Stella's too, although she never seemed to enjoy them much at the time. Now this newcomer seemed to be barging into their gang, sitting on Dorothy's bed as if they were all best friends.

'There aren't any,' she said.

'Oh, come on,' said Letitia. 'Your dad's a criminal lawyer, your mum wrote detective stories. You can do better than that.'

Justice remembered that Letitia's father had known her dad's name. She obviously knew about Mum too. That didn't make Justice like the new girl any better.

'There's nothing going on,' she said. 'Usually there's some mystery with a new member of staff or a new matron, but everyone seems quite boring this term.'

'Except Mr Davenport,' said Letitia. 'He's not boring. He's crackers, if you ask me.'

'Is he the art master?' said Dorothy. 'I thought he was nice. He thanked me for cleaning the studio. Most of the teachers don't even notice the maids are there.'

'He's OK,' said Justice. 'Maybe all the girls will start adoring him instead of Monsieur Pierre.' She stopped, remembering something. 'Dorothy, is there a new gardener?'

'Oh,' said Dorothy, 'you mean Ted. He lives in the village. Why are you asking about him?'

'I saw Helena talking to him,' said Justice. 'Flicking her hair around and flirting like anything.'

'Is that the head girl?' said Letitia. 'I thought she was awful.'

Again, this was roughly what Justice thought too but she felt strangely insulted when Letitia said it. She almost wanted to defend Helena.

'What do you think of the new matron?' she asked Dorothy.

But Dorothy had her head cocked, listening. Then Justice heard it too.

Footsteps. Coming in their direction.

CHAPTER 7

Justice tiptoed to the door. Gesturing to the others to be quiet, she squatted down to look under the door, where there was a large, draughty gap. She could see feet in green high-heeled shoes coming towards them. They stopped by Dorothy's door for what seemed like an age and then, thankfully, continued along the corridor. Justice heard a door open and shut. Then, silence.

'Who was it?' whispered Letitia.

'Miss de Vere,' said Justice. She had recognised the shoes.

'What's she doing up here?' said Dorothy. 'This corridor only leads to the North Turret room, and that's empty.'

'I don't know,' said Justice. 'But I'm going to find out.'

Once before, she had heard voices in the North Turret

room and it had turned out to be Miss de Vere sending radio messages. Was that what she was doing this time? And, if so, why was she doing it in the middle of the night?

'I'll come with you,' said Letitia.

'Me too,' said Dorothy.

'No,' said Justice. 'Three people will make too much noise.' She was thinking of Dorothy. If Justice got caught, she'd get into trouble; Dorothy could lose her job. But, from Dorothy's face, Justice could see that her feelings were hurt. She thought Justice was choosing Letitia over her. Well, there was no time to explain now.

Justice crept along the corridor, Letitia just behind her. She could hear two voices coming from the turret room. Miss de Vere must be using wireless transmission to talk to someone. Dad had explained it once. Justice didn't quite understand it all but she knew that an Italian called Guglielmo Marconi had invented a way of communicating via radio waves. It was this invention that had saved some of the people on board the *Titanic*, which sunk twelve years before Justice was born.

Who was Miss de Vere talking to? It sounded like a man. Justice edged closer and heard Miss de Vere say, 'The situation is desperate now. I'm scared of what he might do.'

Miss de Vere was scared. This made Justice feel scared in turn.

'He can't hurt you now,' said the man, 'not when—'

'Justice Jones!'

Justice turned and found herself face to face with Miss Macintosh, the new matron. Letitia pulled a face behind Matron's back. Justice couldn't help smiling.

'What are you grinning at?' said Matron. 'This isn't a laughing matter, I assure you. You and Letitia are to report to me before breakfast tomorrow. Now, go straight back to bed.'

Justice and Letitia scurried back along the corridor. Dorothy's door was closed and there was no sound from the turret room.

'Two order marks and a hundred lines,' said Justice, as she joined the Barnowls' table at breakfast. 'I must not leave the dormitory at night.'

'I'm going to write "I must leave the dormitory at night",' said Letitia. 'No one will notice.'

Matron had still been angry when Justice and Letitia reported to her that morning. She'd asked what they'd been doing but, before Justice could speak, Letitia had said, 'It was my fault. I dared Justice to go up to the North Turret after lights out.'

'It is strictly forbidden to leave your dormy at night,' said Matron. 'Justice, I'm disappointed in you. As a third year, you should know better. And I understand that you're form captain too. You should be setting a better example. Games of dare are extremely dangerous. Justice, you will receive two order marks and Letitia one, because I make allowances for her being new. Like me.' And she had actually smiled at Letitia.

'It's all right,' Letitia said carelessly. 'I should have two as well.'

'Very well,' said Matron, pursing her lips angrily.

Now Letitia was telling the story. 'It was a great lark,' she said. 'Me and Justice decided to visit Dorothy. I really like Dorothy. Then we heard voices in the North Turret and we decided to investigate. Matron caught us with our ears to the door.'

'How thrilling,' said Eva. 'You're as brave as Justice, Letitia, and she's the bravest person ever.'

'Weren't you scared of ghosts?' said Nora. 'Wait till I tell you the story of the Haunted Tower.'

'Not with Justice as my partner in crime,' said Letitia.

'Well, I think it was a stupid thing to do,' said Rose.

'So do I,' said Stella.

'Stella!' Justice stared at her friend.

'It was really stupid,' said Stella. 'You could have got Dorothy into trouble.'

'She was all right,' said Justice. 'Matron didn't see her. Wait until you hear about the voices I heard . . .'

'I'm not interested,' said Stella. 'I'm going to the prep room now.' And she got up, carried her half-eaten porridge to the swill bucket, and left the dining room.

The Barnowls were stunned into silence. Stella was the calm one, the one who never lost her temper. And now she was storming off before breakfast was even properly over.

Justice felt tears coming to her eyes. She didn't want to be Letitia's partner in crime. She wanted to talk to Stella. To tell her that she had recognised the man's voice in the turret room.

It had been Dad.

CHAPTER 8

Stella didn't speak to Justice all day. Stella wasn't exactly ignoring her – she just made sure that she was always talking to someone else in the line, at recess and at lunch. Justice and Stella sat together in most lessons but you couldn't really chat in class. When Justice asked her a question, Stella answered politely and carried on with her work. There's nothing lonelier, Justice discovered, than sitting beside a friend who was acting like a stranger.

After lunch they had art, and trooped upstairs to the studio. Stella walked on ahead with Irene, so Justice was left with Letitia. She'd tried to keep her distance from Letitia all day – she didn't want Stella to think she was suddenly best friends with her – but now she was so miserable that she welcomed a friendly word from anyone.

'Wonder what mad Mr Davenport will have in store for us today,' said Letitia.

'He'll probably make us draw pictures of spiders and earwigs,' said Justice. 'Seeing the beauty in nature and all that.' Letitia laughed louder than the joke deserved and Stella turned round to look at them. Then she whispered something to Irene, who giggled.

Mr Davenport was sitting at his easel. As usual, he ignored them until they were sitting down, and then he looked up and said, 'Draw me.'

The girls all stared at him.

'Draw me,' said Mr Davenport. 'You have to get used to drawing faces. Remember, eyes are lower down in the face that you think they are. Don't flatter me, though there will be a prize for the person who makes me look the most handsome.'

He didn't smile, so they didn't know if this was a joke or not.

Justice found it very disconcerting trying to draw a real person. Mr Davenport seated himself on a chair in front of them and stared into the middle distance. Justice started with his hair, then realised that she hadn't left enough room for the face. She started again, sketching the face first, but then the eyes were uneven and the nose seemed to wander off to the left. But there was no time for a third attempt because Mr Davenport said, without moving his lips, 'Ten minutes remaining.'

Justice sketched Mr Davenport's beard, which was pointed, like pictures of men in Tudor times. Then she added more hair. The resulting portrait did not look like any human being she had ever seen. The eyes were wonky, the nose was weird and the beard was much darker than the hair. Justice was definitely not going to win the 'most handsome' prize. She glanced at Letitia's work and couldn't suppress a snort of laughter. Letitia had simply drawn a circle with a beard at the bottom. Now she added cross eyes and a piggy nose.

Mr Davenport was walking around examining sketchbooks. When he got to Justice, he said, 'You need to look harder.' He passed Letitia's effort without comment. Then he walked to the front of the class and held up Eva's sketch. Justice gasped, because Eva's drawing actually looked like a real person – Mr Davenport, in fact. She had captured the art teacher's slightly amused expression and his air of looking past them as if spotting something more interesting on the horizon.

'Eva,' said Mr Davenport. 'You are the artist of the day. You win the prize.'

Eva looked thrilled, even when an actual prize did not seem to be forthcoming.

'Your homework is to draw each other,' said Mr Davenport. 'I want a portrait from each of you by the next lesson. Class dismissed.'

'Can I draw you, Justice?' asked Letitia.

'All right,' said Justice. She wasn't looking forward to a portrait of herself as a pig, but no one else seemed to be offering to work with her. Stella and Irene had already left the studio.

In prep, Justice started a letter to Dad. Could she ask if he'd heard from Miss de Vere recently? But what if Miss Macintosh read all their letters, as a previous matron used to do, and then told the headmistress? Justice thought of the words she'd overheard last night.

'The situation is desperate now. I'm scared of what he might do . . .'

'He can't hurt you now, not when—'

Who was the 'he' that they had been talking about? And why was Miss de Vere telling Dad about him? Was this why the headmistress had wanted to talk to Herbert on the first day of term? There were so many questions in Justice's head that she didn't know how to put them in a letter.

In the end, she just wrote:

> *Dear Dad,*
>
> *It seems strange being back at school. I'm Form Captain Couldn't quite believe it when Miss de Vere announced it. We've got a new matron and she seems nice. (She thought she'd better say this, just in case.) We've also got a new art teacher and he makes us draw trees and things. I've made friends with Letitia – the girl on the horse! I wonder how her father knew your name? Can't wait to see you on the half holiday. I've got lots of questions for you . . .*

She hoped that this would make Dad guess that something was up. She wrote a few more lines about school and added a PS. *'Can you send a tuck box?'* Then she put the letter in an envelope. Across the room, she saw Stella doing her Latin homework. She was sharing a dictionary with Irene. Rose and Alicia were whispering together. Letitia was reading a comic concealed in a history textbook, and Eva was drawing.

'Justice!' hissed someone. Justice hoped it was Stella but, to her surprise, Rose was leaning over from her desk and holding out a page torn from a magazine. 'The mater sent me this,' she said. 'Apparently it was in *Lady About Town* a few months ago.' 'The mater' was what Rose called her mother. She seemed just the sort of person who would read a magazine called *Lady About Town*.

The article showed a woman in a huge hat and a man in a bow tie.

'*The Hon Letitia Blackstock,*' Justice read, '*daughter of Lord and Lady Blackstock (pictured above) is due to start at Highbury House Boarding School for the Daughters of Gentlefolk next term. The school, whose head teacher is Miss Dolores de Vere, author of several books about Jane Austen, is an exclusive establishment on the Kent coast.*'

Exclusive? thought Justice. *That's one word for it.*

'Fancy Letitia being an Hon,' whispered Rose. She sounded very impressed. Perhaps Rose would now become Letitia's best friend. At least that would take the pressure off Justice.

'Fancy,' muttered Justice.

'Rose, Justice,' said Helena Bliss, who was taking prep whilst reading *Film Monthly*. 'No talking. Justice, haven't you got some lines to be getting on with?'

Justice sighed and started to write.

I must not leave the dormitory at night.
I must not leave the dormitory at night.
I must not leave the dormitory at night . . .

That evening, Justice wrote in her journal.

Things to do
1. *Make friends with Stella again.*
2. *Find out what Miss DV and Dad were talking about.*
8. *Learn how to draw pictures of people.*

Number 1 was by far the most important.

CHAPTER 9

Justice woke up determined to start the day in a positive frame of mind.

'Good morning, Stella,' she said, looking over the partition between their beds. 'It's a lovely day.'

'Is it?' said Stella. But she smiled and looked more like her usual self.

'Cross-country club this evening,' said Justice. 'Are you looking forward to it?'

'Yes,' said Stella, 'but I haven't run anywhere for weeks. I'll probably collapse before we get to the end of the field.'

They both laughed and the day (which was actually grey and overcast) suddenly seemed brighter. Then Letitia said, from her bed by the window, 'Can I join cross-country club? Anything to get out of this dump for a bit.'

Stella's smile disappeared. 'You'll have to ask Miss Heron,' she said. And she picked up her sponge bag and headed for the bathroom.

After that, Stella retreated back into her shell. As the Barnowls clattered downstairs to breakfast, Justice kept at the back of the group so as to avoid Letitia. In the refectory corridor, she was rewarded by the sight of Dorothy, carrying a jug of milk from the kitchen.

'Dorothy! I didn't see you yesterday. We need to talk about the voices in the North Turret.'

But Dorothy's voice was cold. 'Do we? I thought you had Letitia to talk to.'

'Dorothy!' The injustice of it made Justice feel quite faint. She leant against the wall. 'I didn't ask Letitia to come! She just followed me.'

'You told me to wait in my room,' said Dorothy.

'Because I didn't want you to get into trouble.'

'That's never bothered you before. We've always done things together. But now you've got Letitia.'

'No . . . Dorothy . . .' Justice didn't know what to say – something that hardly ever happened to her. While she stuttered, Dorothy continued on her way to the refectory.

Justice followed a few seconds later, to be greeted by

Helena Bliss, carrying a plate containing a miniscule slice of toast.

'Take an order mark for being late for breakfast, Justice.'

Another order mark. She'd be in double figures by the weekend at this rate. The dormy with the fewest order marks got a treat at the end of term. The Barnowls had never won, a fact for which Rose – with some justification – never failed to blame Justice.

But, when she got to her place, all Justice's troubles seemed to vanish. There was a letter from Dad! They had only been back three days and he'd already written to her. She tore open the envelope.

Dear Justice,

I'm so sorry to send you disappointing news. I have an important trial coming up and I've just learnt that the date clashes with the half-term holiday. I'm so sorry. You know I would change it if I could but judges are not known for their flexibility. Maybe you could go out with Stella and her family? Sending you lots of love and a huge tuck box.

Dad

Justice knew that she couldn't stay in the refectory, with all the Barnowls staring at her and the clatter of mealtime around her, for one more second. She got to her feet and ran out of the room. The great hall was deserted, the suits of armour looking poised, as if ready to come to her aid. Or attack her. Where could she go? The common room? But there was always someone barging in before lessons looking for a lost book. The dormy? But the dormitories were out of bounds during the day and she didn't want another order mark. She glanced towards the main doors. They were bolted shut but the small inner door was open. Suddenly, Justice wanted to be outside, to be away from the oppressive walls of Highbury House where everyone, it seemed, was determined to misunderstand her. Justice sprinted across the hall and out of the door.

The huge oak tree outside had shed more of its leaves and the lawn was red and gold. Justice ran around the side of the house, past the pig sties and the ice house. Through the morning mist she could see the Tower, surrounded by trees. For a moment, she was tempted to hide there. Surely no one would look for her in the Haunted Tower? But then she remembered Nora's ghost story: 'In the Tower, no one could hear her scream.' She needed somewhere nearer and less spooky to hide.

Just beyond the kitchen garden was a wooden building known as the Old Barn. Justice had never seen anyone go inside, but she assumed that it was used to store garden equipment and hay for the pigs. One of the slatted doors was slightly open. Justice crept inside and, in the musky darkness, threw herself on a hay bale to cry.

She had reached the sobbing and hiccoughing stage of crying when the door opened and a man's voice said, 'Who's there?'

Justice sat up. 'Me,' she said stupidly.

The man came nearer. It was the new gardener. What had Dorothy called him? Ted? He was carrying a trowel and a trug full of potatoes.

'Best get back to the house, miss,' said Ted. His voice was kind. 'Lessons are about to start.'

Justice got up and rubbed her eyes. There was hay on her brown skirt and she brushed it off, trying to control her breathing as she did so. Ted watched her for a moment and then said, 'When things get to me, miss, I always tell myself, "Tomorrow will be better." It helps. Try it.'

'Thank you.' Justice was embarrassed now. She edged past the gardener and started to walk back to the school. Would Stella be worried about her? Maybe she was looking for her in the grounds? But, as Justice got nearer the house, she saw another figure waiting for her.

'Justice,' said Letitia. 'What's up?'

Justice told her.

'Don't worry,' said Letitia, linking arms with her. 'You can come out with me and my people on the half holiday. We live quite near so we can go home for the day. You can ride Cloud if you like.'

Justice thought of the terrifying, rearing horse and of spending the half holiday at the home of Lord and Lady Blackstock, rather than having a day out with Stella's noisy, exuberant family. But she was grateful to Letitia for comforting her, and hurt that Stella hadn't come after her.

She found herself saying yes.

CHAPTER 10

'Are you really going to Letitia's for the half holiday?'

It was recess, and the girls were meant to be marching around the courtyard but there were no teachers about and so Justice and Stella had sneaked back into the house. They were standing by the radiator. It was a rounded metal affair that only ever got lukewarm, but it was better than nothing.

'Well, she asked me,' said Justice. She was feeling rather embarrassed about the whole thing. The Barnowls, who'd all seen Justice running out of the dining hall, were being suspiciously nice to her. Stella's voice was kind, but Justice thought that she also seemed rather offended by Justice's choice.

'You could have come with us. You know you could. Dad's got a new car. We're going to drive in to Rye.'

But you didn't ask me, thought Justice. It was Letitia who had come after her.

'I can't really say no now,' she said.

'I suppose not,' said Stella. 'You'll have a great time with Letitia. You might even ride one of the famous horses.'

Justice laughed but she still thought Stella didn't sound entirely friendly. How could she make this right? She didn't think she could stand not seeing Dad and also losing her best friend. She was still wondering what to say when Letitia came bounding up.

'Hi, Justice! Look what I've made.' It was a fake beard made from black cardboard that fitted over her ears. 'Don't I look like Mr Davenport? I'm going to wear it in art and see what he says.'

Justice couldn't help laughing. Letitia looked so funny with a pointed beard – and she did look oddly like the art master.

'That's priceless,' she said. 'Isn't it, Stella?'

But Stella had walked away.

Letitia wore her fake beard in art but Mr Davenport just said, 'A great improvement, Letitia,' so she took it off. She had more success in English where she sneezed every time Miss Crane said 'Shakespeare'. The girls were helpless with laughter by the end of the lesson. But Justice glanced at Stella and saw that her friend wasn't smiling.

Justice wrote to her dad to say that she understood about the trial and that she was going to spend the half holiday with Letitia. A week later, a monster tuck box was delivered during breakfast. The Barnowls were in raptures over the fruit cake, biscuits, sweets and tins of pineapple chunks and peach slices.

'Let's have a you-know-what tonight,' said Eva.

'A what?' said Letitia.

'A – you know! M.I.D.N.I . . .' Eva stopped, getting stuck on the spelling of 'midnight'.

'What's the point of spelling it out?' said Rose. 'Everyone can read.'

'What *is* she spelling out?' said Letitia.

'Midnight feast,' said Justice. 'We eat the food at night, when we're meant to be asleep.'

'What's the point of that?' said Letitia.

'It's fun,' said Rose. 'F.U.N.' she spelt out pointedly.

'If you say so,' said Letitia.

Justice was carrying the hamper out of the dining hall when she saw Dorothy on her way to collect the dirty plates. Here, at last, was a chance to talk to her friend.

'My dad sent me a tuck box,' she said. 'I'm just taking it

up to the dormy.' Helena Bliss had made a special trip over to the Barnowls table to tell Justice that the box would be confiscated if she didn't put it away.

'That's nice,' said Dorothy.

'My dad's not coming for the half holiday,' said Justice. 'So he sent this. To apologise, I suppose.'

Dorothy's eyes softened. 'I'm sorry,' she said. 'Why isn't he coming?'

'He's got a trial and the date can't be changed.'

'Well, I suppose that is his job. He wouldn't let you down otherwise.' Dorothy knew Dad and understood about his work. The thought made Justice feel very close to Dorothy suddenly.

'What are you doing, Justice?' It was Letitia. 'You'll be late for Latin. Not that it matters. Miss Bathurst is half-dead anyway. I don't think she'd notice.'

'I'm just talking to Dorothy,' said Justice, hoping that Letitia would leave them alone.

'Why don't you give Dorothy some biscuits from the hamper?' said Letitia. 'I bet she never gets to eat nice things.'

She meant it kindly, Justice was sure, but Dorothy gave them a reproachful look and hurried away into the hall. Justice took the tuck box up to the dormitory.

*

That night they waited until Matron had passed by on her rounds and then they unpacked the food and started to eat. They toasted Justice's dad in barley water but, though she grinned and said, 'Thanks,' Justice didn't feel as pleased as she usually did when she'd provided the feast. Stella looked over and smiled as if she understood. 'You'll see him soon,' she whispered.

Justice waited until she was back in bed before checking under the Grenadier Guards biscuit tin for the usual note from Dad.

> *Dearest Justice,*
> *Sorry not to see you over the half holiday but I hope you have a good time with Letitia's family. Blackstock Hall is meant to be magnificent. When I see you I will answer all questions, I promise. In the meantime, keep safe even when in search of adventure.*
>
> Veritas et fortitudo
> *All love,*
> *Dad*

How can you promise to answer my questions, thought Justice, *when you don't know what they are?* But the note made her feel very slightly better.

CHAPTER 11

The half holiday was usually the highlight of the term. Justice would tick off the days in her diary, longing for the time when she'd see Dad again. But now it was just another date.

Justice and Stella were friends again, except that something wasn't the same. They sat together in lessons and prep but they didn't have all their old jokes and, in recess, they joined one of the groups of giggling girls rather than standing together, chatting and gossiping. Justice hadn't spoken to Dorothy since their conversation outside the dining hall. She'd sent Dorothy a note but hadn't had an answer and, when she saw her friend around the school, cleaning or carrying coals for the fires, Dorothy avoided her eyes.

There were some excitements, though. The end-of-term

pantomime was to be *Hansel and Gretel.* Justice auditioned and was pleased – and surprised – to get the part of Hansel. The only downside was that Rose was Gretel. Helena Bliss, who normally got all the lead roles, was apparently too busy to take part. A sixth-former called Chona was the witch and Stella was a villager. Cross-country club continued and Justice found that, when she was running, she forgot her troubles for a while. Miss Heron was pleased with her progress and talked about having another inter-school competition before Christmas.

When the half holiday finally came it was a bright and breezy day. 'That's great,' said Letitia, as they waited in the assembly hall for the parents, 'it means we can go out for a ride.' Justice agreed hollowly. She was feeling rather nervous about the proposed horse riding.

Justice saw Stella's parents coming in, smiling and trailing children as usual. Stella's mum gave Justice a hug and Justice wished that she was going out with them in their new car, and not Letitia and the scary horses. Then there was Rose's mother, blonde and glamorous, accompanied by her Important Diplomat husband, who never seemed to smile. Nora's parents, her father with the same lop-sided glasses as his daughter. Eva's mother, chattering away. Helena Bliss, arm-in-arm with a woman who looked about the same age as her. The girls whose parents couldn't come, like Chona whose family lived in Kenya, were drifting off towards the library and common rooms. Perhaps Letitia's parents weren't coming? Justice cheered up at the thought. She could spend the afternoon reading a murder mystery, perhaps one of her mum's Leslie Light books. But then the doors opened and a large man with a moustache and monocle appeared. He looked vaguely familiar from *Lady About Town* but quite unlike the man she had seen on horseback on the first day of term

Miss de Vere hurried over to greet him. 'How lovely to see you, Lord Blackstock.' Justice had never heard the headmistress sounding so flustered.

'Afternoon, Miss de Vere,' said Lord Blackstock. 'Ah, there you are, Letty. Let's go. Andrews is waiting outside in the Rolls.'

'This is Justice,' said Letitia. 'She's coming with us.'

Justice felt acutely embarrassed. She had assumed that Letitia had already written to ask her parents if Justice could come. But Letitia's father just shrugged and said, 'How do you do, Justice,' before turning and striding out of the room. Letitia and Justice followed him.

The Rolls was the most comfortable car Justice had ever been in. Lord Blackstock sat in the front beside Andrews and the girls had the luxurious, cream-cushioned back seat all to themselves. But Justice couldn't help thinking about Dad's car – a Lagonda they called Bessie – and how they would have talked all the time as Dad drove, telling each other all the news. Letitia seemed to have nothing to say to her father.

The car purred across the marshes. They drove through Rye, the houses leaning in towards each other as if they were chatting, and then they were in the country again, bowling along a straight, tree-lined road.

'This is the park,' said Letitia.

'You mean you own all this?' said Justice.

'Yes,' said Letitia carelessly. 'Look, there's the hall.'

In the distance was a sprawling mansion that grew bigger and bigger as they approached. Dad had been right when he said Blackstock Hall was magnificent. The house was built of honey-coloured stone and its windows glittered in the afternoon sun like a hundred eyes. As they got nearer, Justice saw that the building was shaped like a capital E, having two wings jutting out at each end. Stone steps led up to an entrance flanked with pillars.

The Rolls came to a halt and Andrews got out to open the doors for them.

'Let's go to see the horses,' said Letitia.

'Don't you want to say hallo to your mum first?' said Justice. She wanted to put off riding for as long as possible and, besides, she couldn't imagine not wanting to see your mother. If her mum was at home, waiting for her . . . But she couldn't let herself think like that.

Letitia hesitated. 'Oh, all right. Let's find Ma.'

She led the way up the steps and into a hall, far bigger than the great hall at Highbury House. A sweeping staircase led upwards and branched off in two directions.

'She's probably in the library,' said Letitia. 'It's up here.'

They climbed the stairs and walked along a gallery lined with oil paintings. There were people in Elizabethan ruffs, in Victorian crinolines, in uniforms from long-forgotten wars and . . . 'Letitia! Is that you?'

Justice stopped before a picture of a dark-haired girl with a puppy in her arms.

Letitia laughed. 'Yes. That was when I was six. I was an awfully plain child, really. My parents even sacked the first artist because he made me look too ugly.'

But Justice was impressed. She'd never met anyone who had an actual portrait of themselves. The next painting showed a man and a woman standing on the steps in front of the hall. They both looked as stiff as if they'd been carved from stone.

'Ma and Pa when they first inherited the place,' said Letitia. She pushed open a door, shouting, 'Ma! Are you there?'

They were in a book-lined room. Light streamed in through the mullioned windows, illuminating a piano, several battered leather sofas and a woman rising from the window seat.

'Darling! I didn't hear you arrive.'

Letitia's mother was tall and elegant, with dark hair in a bun. Justice was relieved to note that she also seemed very nice. Lady Blackstock said that she was delighted to meet Justice and that any friend of Letitia's was very welcome.

'I've asked Cook to make you an enormous tea,' she said. 'Letty tells me that the food at school is horrid.'

'It is,' said Justice.

'Justice calls the pudding "dead baby",' said Letitia.

'Justice . . .' said Lady Blackstock. 'Justice . . . Oh, you're Veronica Burton's daughter, aren't you? I absolutely love her books. I've got all of them here in the library.'

Justice rarely met anyone who'd heard of Mum. People usually said, 'You're the daughter of Herbert Jones KC.' Miss de Vere had once told her that she liked her mum's books but lately the headmistress only seemed concerned with Dad. Hearing Lady Blackstock talk about Mum in such a warm, interested way almost brought tears to Justice's eyes.

'I like them too,' she managed to say.

'I love the way Leslie Light solves the crimes just by sitting and thinking,' said Lady Blackstock. 'So clever. Your mum must have been a very special lady.'

'She was,' Justice croaked.

Lady Blackstock seemed to realise that it was time to change the subject. 'What do you want to do, girls? Explore the house? Go for a walk in the woods? There are some new deer in the park. You might see them.'

'We're going for a ride,' said Letitia.

Oh dear, thought Justice.

CHAPTER 12

The stables were almost as big as the house. They were arranged around a courtyard and, on every side, horses' heads were poking out.

'Is that Cloud?' said Justice. 'The white one?'

'He's grey because he's got brown eyes,' said Letitia. 'Only albino horses are white. They've got pink eyes.'

Cloud certainly looked white to Justice and extremely beautiful with his flowing mane and tail. He also seemed very spirited, tossing his head and stamping his hooves when the groom led him out of his stable. Justice was relieved that she was going to ride a pony called Rebel. 'He's easier for a beginner,' said Letitia. 'He's tiny. Practically a Shetland.'

Letitia had lent Justice some riding breeches and boots.

They made her feel quite swaggery and confident. This feeling lasted until Rebel was led out. He was dark brown with a black mane and tail and he was *huge*.

'I thought you said he was little,' said Justice.

'He is,' said Letitia. 'He's only fourteen hands.'

It was a whole new language.

'Hold on to the front and back of the saddle,' said Letitia. 'Put your foot in the stirrup. No, facing his tail. There. Now swing yourself up.'

Justice did as she was told and, rather to her surprise, found herself on Rebel's back. But whatever Letitia said, she seemed a very long way from the ground.

'Hold your reins like this.' Letitia demonstrated. 'With your little finger through like that. Don't let them get too long or Rebel will eat grass. He's very greedy.'

Letitia swung herself on to Cloud's back in one easy movement. She looked wonderful on the white (grey) horse, Justice realised. Completely in control, reins held easily in one hand. Justice felt very insecure on Rebel. The saddle seemed uncomfortably narrow and she had already lost one stirrup.

The groom was looking at her doubtfully.

'Do you want me to come with you, miss?' he said to Letitia. 'I can easily saddle up Troubadour.'

'No, we'll be fine,' said Letitia. 'Justice will soon get the hang of it. Walk on, Cloud.'

Letitia and Cloud led the way through a stone archway. To Justice's relief, Rebel followed without any effort on her part. The horses walked sedately along a pathway between two fields and then Letitia halted by a gate. Rebel immediately started to eat the long grass.

'Pull his head up,' said Letitia. Justice did so. Her hands were already aching. 'We'll have a little trot in this field,' said Letitia. 'Try to rise and fall with the horse. Look down at his shoulder to keep in time.'

Letitia undid the latch and rode Cloud into the gate so that it opened. Rebel went through happily enough but, when he saw the open field, his head went up and his ears went forward. He seemed to tremble slightly.

'Hold on to him,' said Letitia, who was shutting the gate.

But it was too late. Rebel had smelled freedom and he was off, galloping across the grass. At least, Justice thought it was galloping. It seemed faster than she had ever travelled, even in Bessie. All she could do was hang on to Rebel's mane and hope that the pony would get tired soon. It was terrifying: the fields and hedges whooshing past, the wind in her face. Then she heard hooves behind her and Cloud drew alongside.

Letitia reached over and grabbed Rebel's reins. The horses came to a standstill and Justice fell off.

The ground felt extremely hard, but it was a relief to lie still for a few seconds.

'Are you all right?' said Letitia. She dismounted, holding both horses.

'Fine.' Justice stood up and realised that this was true.

'I'm sorry. Rebel hasn't been out for a while and he just got excited. You did really well to stay on when he was galloping. Shall I help you get back on? Give you a leg up?'

'I can manage, I think.' Somehow Justice got her foot in the stirrup and scrambled back into the saddle.

'Do you want to go home?' said Letitia, looking up at her.

'Are you joking?' said Justice. 'This is the best fun ever.'

Letitia laughed and remounted, with difficulty, because Cloud insisted on walking round in circles.

'Let's have a nice, gentle canter then,' she said.

When they dismounted back at the stables, Justice felt her legs almost collapse under her.

'You'll feel stiff at first,' said Letitia. 'But we can have baths back at the house. Here' – she handed Justice some small pellets – 'give Rebel these. He loves them.'

'What are they?'

'Pony nuts. I always carry some with me. Even in my dressing gown.'

Justice could believe this. She held out her hand ('Keep your palm flat,' said Letitia) and Rebel mumbled away at the pony nuts. It tickled but felt marvellous.

'I love Rebel,' she said.

'I'm so glad,' said Letitia. 'You can ride him whenever you come to stay.' And she tucked her hand into Justice's arm as they walked back to the hall.

'Let's have our baths before tea,' said Letitia. 'You can have my bathroom. I'll use Ma's.'

Letitia had her own bathroom? Justice had never heard of such luxury. And it *was* luxurious. The bath stood on its own in the centre of a large, tiled room. The water was blessedly hot after the tepid stuff at Highbury House, and Letitia added some green bath salts which she said were 'wonderful after horse riding'. Justice had to be quick because it was already four o'clock and they had to be back at school at six, but she could have stayed in that scented bath for ever.

The tea was something else, though: sandwiches, sausage rolls, scones with jam and cream, Victoria sponge, iced fairy cakes, chocolate éclairs. The girls ate and ate, while Lady Blackstock ('Call me Pamela, Justice, dear') watched them and laughed.

'I don't believe they feed you at school at all.'

'They don't,' said Letitia, putting a whole fairy cake in her mouth.

'Cook can make up a box of food to take back with you,' said Pamela.

Letitia was too busy eating to answer so Justice said politely, 'Thank you very much, Lady Blackstock . . . Pamela. That would be super.'

When Letitia's mother had left the room, Justice said, 'We can have a midnight feast.'

'So we can. I tell you what, let's have it in the Haunted Tower.'

'The Haunted Tower? Why?'

'Why not? Would be more of a lark than having it in the boring old dormy. We'll ask Nora to tell her ghost story.'

'The others won't agree,' said Justice. 'Eva will be too scared and Rose will say we're breaking school rules.' *And what about Stella?* she thought. She had a feeling that Stella wouldn't like it either.

'Then they needn't come,' said Letitia.

A small cloud seemed to pass over the sunny afternoon.

CHAPTER 13

To Justice's surprise, the other Barnowls seemed quite keen on Letitia's midnight feast idea. Maybe they were just dazzled by the array of food displayed when Letitia opened her wicker hamper.

'That's enough tuck for the whole school,' breathed Eva.

'Well, we're not going to share it with them,' said Letitia. 'I vote we go to the Tower at midnight. It'll be spookier then.'

'The witching hour,' said Nora, her glasses gleaming.

'Won't the Tower be locked?' said Stella. She hadn't said much since they'd all got back from the half holiday, but she ·had asked Justice about her afternoon. Justice had said that it was fine and they'd gone for a ride. She'd left it at that. She didn't think Stella would want to know about the magnificence of Letitia's house or the fact that Justice had, by the end of her visit, completely fallen in love with Rebel and horses in general.

'Ask Justice,' said Rose. 'She's the only one who makes a habit of sneaking out to the Tower after dark.'

'I don't make a habit of it,' said Justice. 'I went once and, yes, the Tower was locked. Hutchins has the key. But I've got another idea. You know the barn near the ice house? I went there the other day and it was open. We can have our midnight feast in there. It's more sheltered than the Tower.'

'Not as spooky though,' objected Letitia.

'Oh, I don't know,' said Nora. 'The ghost of Grace Highbury walks there too. A lonely figure in her white gown, wailing and wringing her hands.'

'Don't, Nora,' said Eva. 'I'm too scared to go now.'

'Don't be wet,' said Rose.

Justice didn't know why Rose was in favour of the plan. Usually, as dormitory captain, she was a stickler for the rules. Maybe she was determined to prove to the Hon Letitia that Highbury House girls had some spirit. Rose had been by the main entrance when Letitia and Justice had returned to the school that afternoon, alighting from the Rolls with effusive thanks on Justice's part and a casual, 'See you, Pa,' on Letitia's. Rose's eyes had narrowed. Justice knew that Rose was very proud of her father's Rolls-Royce and wouldn't want another pupil travelling in such style. 'What was Letitia's house like?' Rose had asked Justice when they queued for Meal. 'Big,' said Justice. 'Her father's Lord Blackstock,' said Rose. 'He's awfully rich, owns loads of factories and things. The pater was telling me about him.' If Rose's father – the pater – was interested in Letitia's family, maybe this explained Rose's change of heart.

'All right,' said Letitia. 'The barn it is. Everyone link hands and say, "We promise to have fun".'

'We promise to have fun,' echoed the Barnowls, as if hypnotised.

It didn't feel so much fun at a quarter to midnight. Justice had put her alarm clock under her pillow and its muffled ring made her sit bolt upright, heart pounding. What was going on? Oh yes, the midnight feast. The room was freezing and she was half tempted to lie down again and pull the blankets over her head.

But, from across the room, Letitia whispered, 'Is it midnight?'

'Ten to,' said Justice.

There was a sliver of light as Letitia twitched back the curtain. 'Full moon,' she said.

Justice got up and shook Stella's shoulder. Stella took a few minutes to wake up. Her face was pale in the moonlight.

'Oh, Justice,' she whispered. 'Is this a good idea?'

'It'll be fine,' said Justice. Although she was far from sure herself.

The Barnowls put on their dressing gowns and outdoor shoes and then Justice led the way along the creaking corridor. Letitia brought up the rear, carrying the hamper. Justice stopped outside Matron's room but everything was quiet. She beckoned to the others to follow.

One of the first things Justice did when she arrived at Highbury House was to draw a map of the rambling building. She had been adding to it over the last year and had discovered a new way into the grounds. The so-called maids' staircase led down to the scullery, where there was a door into the kitchen gardens. This was safer than going via the main stairs and the great hall. They crept down the stone stairs. A sudden noise made Justice stop and Stella cannon into the back of her. The scullery door, which must have been ajar, suddenly opened further and Rudi, the housekeeper's cat, appeared, looking outraged to see humans in his territory. Justice reached out to stroke him but Rudi stalked away, tail held high. Justice pushed the scullery door open further and, followed by the other Barnowls, tiptoed across the room. The drying rack and mangle loomed ominously in the darkness but there was the outside door with the key still in the lock. Justice opened it and put the key in her dressing gown pocket.

'Come on.'

The grounds were silver in the moonlight, the grass crackling with frost. They took the path by the kitchen gardens, the hedges looking huge and sinister in the darkness. Justice looked up at the dark windows of Highbury House. Was anyone watching them? But there were no lights anywhere, not even in the North Turret. She suddenly thought of Dorothy, who would have loved an adventure like this. But Dorothy still wasn't talking to her.

The barn loomed up in front of them and – thank goodness – the door was still open. Justice led the way inside. It was much warmer in there and the straw looked golden in the light of Justice's torch. They arranged the hay bales in a square to provide some protection from the cold night air. Letitia opened the hamper. Suddenly it was fun again.

Letitia handed out cakes and some rather squashed sandwiches. Soon everyone was chomping happily.

'Who made these?' said Rose. 'Your mater?'

'No, the cook,' said Letitia, sounding surprised.

'Do you have lots of servants?'

'Not really. Just a cook and a butler and two maids, you know. And Ma's maid and Pa's valet.'

The girls were momentarily silenced. At home, Justice and her father had Mrs Minchin, who cooked for them and looked after the house. But, when Mum was alive, it had just been the three of them. Justice thought of Blackstock Hall: the sweeping staircase, the portraits, the park with the deer grazing in the woods, the stables full of gleaming horses.

'There are all the grooms too,' she said, without thinking.

'Oh, they're outdoor servants,' said Letitia.

'Do you have lots of ponies?' said Eva.

'I've got one, Cloud. And my old pony, Rebel. Justice rode him today.'

'And fell off,' said Justice.

The girls laughed and started talking about pets. Nora had a spaniel called Mr Frisk. Rose's mother had a Siamese cat called Bella. Justice had met Stella's black cat, Minky, and was glad when Stella started talking about her. She didn't want Letitia to talk as if she and Justice were friends. Well, they were, in a way, and Justice had enjoyed her day at Blackstock Hall. But she would still rather have been with her dad.

After they'd finished eating, Letitia told a joke about a dog eating a sausage roll and Eva laughed so much that she had hiccoughs. Justice glanced at the open door, hoping they weren't making too much noise, but the barn was a long way from the house and the grounds had been deserted. Surely the only living creature out there was Rudi, looking for mice. *All the same*, she thought, *we'd better be a bit quieter.* 'Let's tell stories,' she said.

'Yes,' said Letitia. 'Tell us the Haunted Tower ghost story, Nora.'

It was now quite cosy inside their straw barricade. The remains of the picnic lay in front of them and the torch, propped up by a thermos flask, reflected the beams above. Nora settled herself more comfortably. 'It all begins when this house was owned by an evil man called Lord Highbury. He had a daughter called Grace who was very beautiful, with long blonde hair.'

Justice wasn't looking at Rose but she just *knew* that Rose was flicking her pale plaits complacently.

'Lord Highbury wanted Grace to marry her cousin but she refused. She was in love with the gardener . . .'

'Like Helena Bliss,' Justice whispered to Stella.

Nora raised her voice slightly – she didn't like to be interrupted.

'The gardener was handsome and kind but very poor. Lord Highbury would not hear of his daughter marrying a mere servant. So he shut Grace in the Tower, saying he wouldn't release her until she changed her mind. Alone in the tower, with no food or water, Grace wept bitterly but there was no one to hear her, only the wind and the rain. Eventually Grace was too weak to make a sound and she died, clutching her locket containing an image of the gardener. On dark nights, you can hear her wailing in the Tower and sometimes you can see her walking through the grounds in her white nightdress, looking for her lost love.'

At that moment, a piercing scream rent the night. The Barnowls jumped to their feet, looking at each other wildly.

'It's Grace!' squeaked Eva.

'Nonsense,' said Justice, although she knew that she was trembling. She grabbed her torch and went to the door of the barn, the Barnowls close behind her. The shaky light illuminated dark hedges and frozen grass. In the distance they could see the Tower with the full moon above it and, walking quickly in their direction, a tall figure in a white dress.

The Barnowls panicked. With no thought of anything except getting back to the house, they ran helter-skelter through the gardens until they arrived at the back door.

Somehow Justice found the key in her pocket and fitted it in the lock. They hurtled through the scullery, up the stairs and along the corridor, not caring about the creaking floorboards. And, finally, they were back in their dormy.

The girls looked at each other, somewhere between hysterical laughter and tears.

'That was *terrifying*,' said Stella.

'It was a ghost!' said Eva. 'We saw a ghost!'

'Well, we're safe now,' said Justice.

But Rose was looking around the room.

'Where's Letitia?' she said.

CHAPTER 14

Justice suddenly felt icy cold.

'Letitia was right behind me,' she said.

Or was she? In all honesty, Justice couldn't remember much of the mad dash back through the grounds. She remembered the moon and the ghostly figure, almost gliding over the white grass, then the next thing she recalled was fumbling for the key and leading the girls back up the stairs and along the dormy corridor. Letitia had been with them. Hadn't she?

Justice went to the door. 'She must be out here.' But, as Justice looked out into the corridor, she saw something even more sinister. Matron's light was on.

She dashed back into the dormy but there was no chance to hide. They could all hear footsteps coming in their direction. Instinctively, the Barnowls gathered together in the centre of the room.

The door opened and Matron stood there, wearing a pink, quilted dressing gown over her nightdress, but no less scary for that.

'What's going on?' she said. 'I heard you all running along the corridor. And why are you wearing your outside shoes?'

There was no point trying to hide anything.

'We were having a midnight feast,' said Justice.

'And Letitia is missing,' Eva blurted out. Tears were running down her cheeks.

'Missing?' said Matron. Justice could hear fear in her voice. 'What do you mean, "missing"?'

'She was with us, but she didn't come back to the dormy,' said Justice. 'She's probably still in the grounds.'

'You went into the grounds for a midnight feast?' said Matron. 'Where exactly?'

'The old barn,' said Stella. She linked hands with Justice. It helped. A lot.

'Right,' said Matron. 'You girls stay here. I'm going to get Hutchins and Miss de Vere. You are all in serious trouble.'

No one, not even Eva, doubted that.

*

They waited for what felt like hours. At first Justice was sure that Letitia would come swaggering in at any minute, laughing at having fooled them. But, as light started to filter in through the curtains Letitia had opened, hope started to fade. They all got back into bed, but Justice didn't think anyone slept.

At 5 a.m. Matron came into the room. She was fully dressed and looked very grim.

'The police have been called,' she said. 'You girls are to see Miss de Vere first thing in the morning.'

The police! After Matron had gone, Eva burst into tears. Justice felt like crying too.

'She must be playing a trick on us,' said Rose, again and again. 'Don't you think so, Justice? You're the one who's so pally with her.'

Once, Justice would have protested about this, worried that Stella would be jealous, but now these sorts of worries seemed unimportant.

'She might be playing a trick,' she said. 'But they would have found her by now. The grounds aren't that big.'

She went to the window but their dormy looked out towards the gymnasium and the Tower, not the old barn. The sky was now pale pink and, as she watched, a police car – a black Wolseley – turned into the drive.

'They're here,' she said. 'The police are here.'

It's real, she thought. One of her friends was missing and the police were going to search for her. With a sinking heart, Justice remembered what Letitia had made them say.

We promise to have fun.

The girls were dressed and ready when Miss de Vere came into the dormy at 6 a.m. The headmistress was dressed in a tweed suit with a blue jumper and looked as neat and tidy as ever, but her face was very pale.

Miss de Vere sat on the only chair in the dormy. The Barnowls usually used it to put wet towels on.

'The police want to see you all after breakfast,' she said, 'but first I need you to tell me exactly what happened last night.'

Justice sensed that the others were waiting for her to start.

'We decided to have a midnight feast in the grounds,' she said. 'Letitia had brought some food from home and we thought it would be . . . we thought it would be fun.'

'It was Letitia's idea,' said Rose.

'We all thought it sounded fun,' said Justice.

We promise to have fun.

The headmistress looked as if she was about to speak, but seemed to think better of it and nodded at Justice to continue.

'We woke up at ten to midnight. We went into the grounds by the scullery exit.'

'Wasn't it locked?' said Miss de Vere.

'The key was in the door,' said Justice. 'I took it with me. We went through the gardens to the old barn. We had our picnic then and . . . and chatted.'

'I told a ghost story,' said Nora, sounding apologetic. 'About Grace Highbury.'

'Is that old story still doing the rounds?' said Miss de Vere. 'Even the teachers were talking about it the other day. There's no truth in it. Go on, Justice.'

'After Nora's story, we got frightened. Then we heard a scream. We went to the door of the barn and we thought we saw a woman in the grounds, a woman dressed in white. We ran into the house. We were so scared that it wasn't until we got into the dormy that we realised Letitia wasn't with us.'

'When was the last time you saw Letitia?' said Miss de Vere. 'Think, girls. This is very important.'

'I think it was when Nora was telling the story,' said Justice. 'Letitia asked her to tell it.'

'I thought Letitia was behind me running into the house,' said Eva. 'But I'm not sure now.'

'I thought she said something when we saw the ghost . . . the figure,' said Nora, 'but I don't know.'

'Tell me about the figure,' said Miss de Vere. 'Are you sure you saw it?'

'It was a woman in a long, white dress,' said Justice. 'And it was real. We all saw it.'

The others agreed that they had.

'And did you see anything else, any*one* else, on your escapade? Which, I'm sure I don't have to tell you, was completely against school rules.'

'We didn't see anyone,' said Justice. 'Only Rudi, Mrs Hopkirk's cat.'

'Will we be expelled?' asked Eva.

'You won't be expelled,' said Miss de Vere. 'But you are in serious trouble.'

Justice had heard this so often that it was almost comforting. She sensed that Miss de Vere hadn't quite decided what to do with them and that it wasn't the most important thing on her mind.

'You can go now,' said Miss de Vere. 'I've asked Cook to give you an early breakfast. Then you will be interviewed by Detective Inspector Deacon. Justice, I'd like to speak to you on your own.'

That, Justice thought, *is never a good sign.*

For what felt like ages, Miss de Vere just sat there, looking at Justice very intently. Justice had always thought that the headmistress seemed to be able to see right into her mind. What could she see there now? Fear? Panic? Guilt?

'Justice,' said Miss de Vere at last. 'When you were with the Blackstocks yesterday, did anyone mention your mother's books?'

This was not what Justice was expecting.

'Yes,' she said. 'Lady Blackstock said that she liked them.'

'Anything else?'

Justice tried to think back: the book-lined room, the sun streaming in through the windows, Lady Blackstock rising to greet them. *You're Veronica Burton's daughter, aren't you? I absolutely love her books.*

'She said she liked the way Leslie Light solved the mysteries,' she said. 'By sitting and thinking.'

'Who was there when she said that?'

'Just me and Letitia.'

'Justice' – Miss de Vere leaned forward – 'you know Letitia best. Could this possibly be a prank?'

It was the question Justice had been asking herself all night.

'At first I thought it might be,' she said slowly. 'Letitia does like to . . . surprise people . . . but I don't think she would have stayed out so long. It would be more like her to hide in a cupboard and jump out to give us all a shock.'

Ridiculously, they both looked towards the cupboard at the end of the dormy. But the door didn't open. Letitia didn't appear.

Justice realised that Miss de Vere was holding something out to her.

'This was pushed under my door,' she said. 'I saw it when I came back from searching in the grounds.'

It was a page torn out of a book. All the words had been inked out except for a few.

I Have taken Her

Justice looked at the title at the top of the page.

Murder in the Mansion. Written by Veronica Burton.

CHAPTER 15

Justice ate cold porridge in the empty refectory and then Matron escorted her to the staff room, where Detective Inspector Deacon was waiting. In ordinary circumstances, Justice would have been fascinated to see inside this room, which was normally out of bounds to pupils. The nearest she had ever come was standing outside to deliver a message, and she'd got a tantalising glimpse of a roaring fire, cosy armchairs and velvet curtains. There was no fire in the grate now, and the curtains were drawn back to reveal a dull, grey sky.

Inspector Deacon stood up when she entered, which Justice thought was unnecessarily polite. The inspector was tall and grey-haired with a soft voice that nevertheless had a definite note of command. Justice had met him once before and had been impressed by his casual air of being in control of even the stickiest situation. It was a relief to see him now.

'Sit down, Justice,' said the inspector. 'Thank you, Matron. You can leave us now.'

Matron closed the door quietly. Listening to her footsteps descending the staircase, Justice suddenly felt nervous and rather guilty. She understood why people confessed things to police officers. She felt like confessing, even though she didn't know what for.

'So, Justice,' said Inspector Deacon with a slight smile. 'We meet again.'

'Yes,' said Justice. 'Inspector.' She didn't know what to call him and it seemed a cheek to say nothing.

'Tell me what happened last night,' said Inspector Deacon.

Justice told him about the midnight feast, the ghost story and the flight through the gardens. She assumed that the other girls would have told him exactly the same story. The inspector didn't look at her when she was speaking – he was gazing out of the window – but she knew that he was listening intently. When she had finished, he said, 'Tell me about the ghostly figure.'

Justice had been trying to remember this all morning. She didn't need the detective to tell her that this apparition, far from being a ghost, was probably the person who had abducted Letitia.

'The person was tall,' she said. 'Wearing a long dress.' She knew that this was a very poor description, unworthy of a sleuth but, at the time, she'd been too scared to notice much.

'We've undertaken a thorough search of the grounds,' said the inspector. 'We found the remains of a picnic in the Old Barn – some field mice were having quite a feast – and footprints leading to and from the house. Unfortunately, there are so many that it was impossible to examine them properly. We did find this, though.'

The inspector held something out to her. It was a scrap of white material. *Brocade*, she thought, embroidered with tiny white flowers.

'We found this caught on one of the rose bushes,' said Inspector Deacon. 'Could it be from the dress?'

'I didn't get a close look at it,' said Justice, 'but I suppose so.'

'Think back,' said the inspector. 'Did the figure have long hair? Blonde or dark?'

This was difficult too because, in Justice's memory, the figure had long, blonde hair like Grace Highbury. But was this really true?

'I don't know,' she said. 'I don't really remember the hair.'

'It was tall, you say. Could it have been a man?'

This, too, had occurred to Justice.

'Yes,' she said. 'It could have been a man.'

'You've heard that Miss de Vere has received a ransom note torn from one of your mother's books?'

'Yes.' *Ransom note.* This makes the whole thing sound very serious. And had the blacked-out page even mentioned a ransom? Justice didn't think so.

'Has anyone mentioned your mother's books to you recently?'

'Only Lady Blackstock yesterday.' Justice recounted the conversation about Leslie Light.

'Sitting and thinking, eh?' said the inspector. 'Well, there's a bit more to it than that.' He looked at Justice as if coming to a decision. 'Justice, I've spoken to my colleague, Inspector Porlock, of the Yard, about you. We both think that you've got the instincts of a detective. I don't want you to put yourself in any danger but I do want you to keep your eyes and ears open. If you see anything that you think is suspicious, however small, tell me immediately. Is that a deal?'

'Yes,' said Justice.

'Here's my card,' said Inspector Deacon. 'You can telephone me any time.'

Despite everything, Justice could not help feeling rather proud.

As Justice left the staff room, she saw a familiar figure on the landing. Dorothy was dusting the stairs. When she saw Justice she straightened up, came over and gave her a hug.

'I'm so sorry about Letitia. Has she really been kidnapped?'

'I think so. The police are here. I was talking to Inspector Deacon just now. Do you remember him?' Justice was referring to the time last term when they had been trapped by a murderer in a house called Smugglers' Lodge. Inspector Deacon had arrived to make the arrest. She could see Dorothy remembering too.

'Yes. I thought he was like a policeman in a book.'

'I know what you mean.'

'Mrs Hopkirk told Cook that you saw the ghost of Grace Highbury. Is that true?'

Justice knew that Dorothy would enjoy this bit of the story, so she said, 'Yes. We saw a white figure gliding towards us over the grass. It was terrifying.'

Dorothy shivered. 'I wish I'd been there.'

'I wish you'd been there too.'

They smiled at each other and, again, despite the awfulness of the situation, Justice was happy that they were friends again.

'So,' said Dorothy, in a businesslike voice. 'Are there any clues?'

'A few,' said Justice. 'I'm going to write them down in my journal. There's the mysterious figure, for one, and a piece of white material caught on a rose bush. Oh, and Miss de Vere received a ransom note.'

'*No!*'

Justice almost laughed at the expression on Dorothy's face, which was half-shock and half-pure delight.

But then Justice heard footsteps on the stairs and all desire to laugh left her: Miss de Vere was coming towards them, accompanied by Lord and Lady Blackstock. Dorothy pressed herself into the wall, as if trying to make herself invisible. Justice thought this was probably what she did every time a teacher or a pupil passed her. The thought made her uncomfortable. At any rate, the Blackstocks did not seem to notice Dorothy, but they both saw Justice.

'Justice!' Lady Blackstock caught hold of her hand. 'Can you help us? Do you know what happened to Letty?'

'No.' Justice managed to croak. 'I'm sorry. One minute she was there and the next . . . she just wasn't.'

'Justice has told us everything she knows,' said Miss de Vere. But Justice thought the headmistress gave her a sharp look all the same.

'Someone will pay for this,' said Lord Blackstock. He continued down the stairs, his voice echoing through the panelled halls. 'When I find the person responsible, I will destroy them. And I'll get this school closed down.'

Justice looked at Miss de Vere and saw an expression of pure terror on her face.

CHAPTER 16

School had changed overnight. Justice remembered the
other time that a serious crime had occurred at Highbury
House – the way that the teachers had suddenly seemed
scared, and how scared that had made her. It was the same
now that Letitia had vanished. Justice kept seeing teachers
standing in huddles and overhearing things like: 'I always
knew that girl was trouble' (Miss Bathurst). 'It's Dolores I
feel sorry for' (Miss Morris). 'The school might have to
close' (Miss Hunting). '*Sacré bleu!*' (Monsieur Pierre).

The girls were all subdued, but Justice knew that everyone
was staring at her and whispering . . . 'Justice was her friend!'
'Justice must know something about it, wasn't she mixed up
in that other murder?' 'I wouldn't trust that Justice Jones.
Her father's always defending murderers.' In Latin, Justice

111

looked out of the window and saw a line of police officers moving slowly over the lower field. There was even a bloodhound straining at its leash. What were they looking for? Clues, or Letitia's body? The thought made Justice feel slightly sick and she turned back to Catullus with relief.

In art, Mr Davenport asked to see their homework portraits. Justice had drawn Letitia and, although it wasn't a very good likeness, it still gave her a pang to see the drawing. Letitia had insisted on sticking her tongue out and although Justice hadn't drawn her like that, there was a certain cheekiness to Letitia's expression, even though one eye was higher than the other and Justice didn't know how to do hair. The most realistic thing was the bootlace that Letitia used as a ribbon to tie back her hair with, its ends hanging down on either side of her face.

Mr Davenport looked at the picture in silence for a minute. 'That's definitely Letitia,' he said. 'You're not a flatterer, Justice.'

Justice didn't know if this was a compliment or not. Mr Davenport looked at the portrait again and sighed. 'Today,' he said, 'draw yourselves.'

Rose put up her hand. 'Please, sir. We haven't got any mirrors.' There was nothing Rose liked more than looking at herself in mirrors, but there were hardly any at Highbury

House. The glass in the bathroom was so old and spotty that you could hardly see your own reflection.

'No,' said Mr Davenport. 'Exactly.'

Justice stared at her sketchbook. What did she look like? Chin-length brown hair, brown eyes (hazel, Mum used to say), straight nose, freckles. What did she look like to other people? She wasn't a Beauty with a capital letter, like Rose. She was just ordinary-looking, she thought, able to blend into the background, which was ideal for a sleuth. She looked across at Stella, who was looking equally baffled. Justice thought she could easily draw Stella: dark hair pulled back into a ponytail, brown eyes, a mouth that looked serious until she smiled. Stella smiled at her now, which made Justice feel better. At least her two best friends, Stella and Dorothy, had forgiven her.

Justice draw a circle in her book and added eyes, nose and mouth. She didn't think that she would be Mr Davenport's artist of the day.

By the end of the day, the Barnowls were exhausted. After all, they had only slept for a few hours the night before. In the dormy they hardly spoke as they got ready for bed. They all tried to avoid looking at Letitia's empty bed. Justice remembered Letitia's confident voice saying, 'Bagsy the bed by the window.' 'You can't bagsy a bed,' Rose had said. 'You're new.' Letitia was so bold, not daunted by anything, not even by Rose at her most haughty. *Was* it possible that Letitia had actually planned the whole thing? Had she simply run away from school, as Justice had dreamt of doing many times? After all, the midnight feast in the grounds had been Letitia's idea. *We promise to have fun.* But then Justice remembered Lady Blackstock's face when they had met on the stairs that morning. She didn't think that Letitia would want to make her mother so unhappy.

What about Lord Blackstock, though? Justice remembered the silent car journey, the way Letitia had run back into the school without acknowledging her father. Could her disappearance be Letitia's way of getting back at her father for something, or at least getting him to notice her? Justice loved her dad but she sometimes felt that he was more interested in his work than he was in her. This was unfair, she knew, but, all the same, she could imagine Letitia wanting to do something that would make her impassive father sit up and pay attention to her. But Letitia had now been missing for almost a full day. Surely that was taking a joke too far, even for Letitia? Besides, the police had been searching the grounds for hours. They even had a bloodhound with them.

The dog would have found Letitia even if she'd discovered the best hiding place in the world.

Leslie Light always said that the best place to hide something was in plain sight. Could Letitia possibly still be in the house? She could have followed the Barnowls in and then whisked away to some secret hidey-hole. But how had she found such a place when she'd only been at the school for half a term? Justice thought of Letitia saying, 'I'd love to find a secret tunnel, wouldn't you?' There *was* a tunnel, in the cellars, but Miss de Vere had been at pains to tell Justice that it was now boarded up. Could there be another tunnel somewhere in the mysterious house that, as Letitia had pointed out, seemed bigger inside than it did outside. Now Justice could hear Letitia's voice, the night that they'd heard voices in the North Turret. *It's a bit creepy but it would be a great place to hide. No one would think of looking here.* Letitia couldn't be in Dorothy's room, but had she found another hiding place so good that no one would find her there?

Justice's hard, iron-framed bed felt like a luxury couch; all she wanted to do was close her eyes and sleep, but she forced herself to get out her journal. She'd forgotten that she'd left it under her pillow and not in its usual hiding place under the loose floorboard. It was lucky that Matron had been too distracted to do her usual check of the beds.

Justice pulled the covers over her head, switched on her torch and wrote: *The Disappearance of Letitia*. 'Kidnapping' just sounded too horrible.

Clues: (she wrote)

Figure in the grounds. Tall. Possibly a man. Query: hair colour?

White material found on rose bush. Looked expensive. Who would have a dress like that

Note from Mum's book. Who reads Veronica Burton? Check library tomorrow.

Her eyes were closing. She'd have to stop. She closed the journal and, as she did so, noticed a piece of paper trapped in the pages. Justice smoothed it out. It was a page from *Murder in Milan*, a Leslie Light mystery set in Italy.

All the words on it had been crossed out except: *Tower midnight Tomorrow. don't Tell.*

CHAPTER 17

Don't tell. The words echoed in Justice's head all night and all the next day. Inspector Deacon had told her to contact him if she saw anything suspicious. *If you see anything that you think is suspicious, however small, tell me immediately.* An anonymous note was definitely not a small thing. Should she tell the inspector? Should she tell Miss de Vere? But what if the note-writer found out and did something awful to Letitia? It would be all Justice's fault.

Justice couldn't forget something that had happened almost a year ago. She'd received a note, supposedly from Dorothy, asking her to meet at the Tower. Justice had duly gone to the Tower, only to be confronted by a killer. What if this was also a trap? Was it significant that this message suggested the same meeting place? And why was the letter-writer using pages from Mum's books? There had to be some reason for it all.

She couldn't concentrate during maths but Miss Morris seemed to accept that they were all upset and wasn't as strict as usual. She even let Eva get away with describing the hypotenuse as a hippopotamus. Miss Crane was equally understanding in English. When Justice asked if she could go to the library to change her reading book, she just told her not to be too long about it.

The library was a rather grand room on the ground floor. However, like a lot of things at Highbury House, it wasn't quite as impressive as it first seemed. The bookshelves reached up to the ceiling but most of the books were never read. Some of them were even kept in locked glass cases, as if they were dangerous animals. Justice had heard that, before Miss de Vere came to the school, there were no modern books at all. But the headmistress, who was an author herself, had bought a few of the latest titles, which were kept on the lower shelves. Justice was slowly reading her way through Agatha Christie. She knew that there were some of her mother's books in the library too, but she'd always been afraid to touch them somehow, and had never seen anyone else reading them. Now she looked for the shelf with authors beginning with B. Barton, Brontë, Brown,

Buchan, . . . There they were, six of them. *Murder in the Mansion. Mission to Murder. We Are For the Dark. Blood Will Have Blood. Murder in Milan.* There was even a copy of *Murder in the Library.*

Justice picked up *Murder in Milan.* She assumed that it had been chosen because it featured the Leaning Tower of Pisa and so had the word 'tower' in it. When you took a book out of the library you were supposed to write the date on the ticket kept inside the front cover, and put the ticket in a special box. There was no librarian but Miss Crane sometimes checked. The last date on this ticket was 4 May 1936, a few months before Justice had first come to the school. She flicked through the pages until she came to the one that had been ripped out to make the message that had been left in her journal. There were no missing pages. This meant that the kidnapper hadn't used the library copy. But, as Leslie Light always said, 'A negative does not prove a positive.' The letter-writer could still be someone at the school. *Could* it be Letitia herself? This idea was still at the back of Justice's mind. Letitia knew about Mum's books. This could be her idea of an elaborate prank.

If so, it was another reason not to tell Inspector Deacon or Miss de Vere about the note.

Justice decided. She would go to the Tower at midnight.

She would be careful, would just observe and, at the first sign of danger, she would run back to the house. The hardest thing was deciding not to tell Stella and Dorothy. But the letter-writer had said 'don't tell' and, for all she knew, it could be someone nearby, someone who was watching her at this very moment. Justice shivered and looked around the room. But the library was empty, the rows of leather-bound books looking down at her, heavy with knowledge.

Justice went back to English. She was so quiet that Miss Crane asked if she had a headache.

'Shall I take her to sick bay?' asked Eva eagerly.

'No, thank you, Eva,' said Miss Crane. 'Get on with your reading.'

'Can we practise for the pantomime?' asked Rose.

Please say no, Justice begged the teacher silently. The last thing she wanted was to act out *Hansel and Gretel* with Rose. Perhaps Miss Crane felt the same because she said, 'We'll practise next lesson. Let's just stay quiet for today.'

It was shepherd's pie for lunch. This was a favourite with the students despite, Justice thought, tasting as if it had been made with actual shepherds. The girls all ate heartily, jostling over second helpings. Only the Barnowls were distracted, aware of the other tables looking at them and whispering. Rose was swishing her hair defiantly, Stella looked worried and Eva confused. Nora was obviously torn between worry and the desire to make a great story out of Letitia's disappearance.

'Are you all right, Justice?' said Stella. 'You've hardly eaten anything.'

'I'm OK,' said Justice. 'Oh, look out. Helena's coming over.'

The Barnowls sat up straighter as the head girl drifted across the room. She looked as glamorous as ever, hair loose about her shoulders (the strict rule about tying back hair obviously did not apply to Helena); but Justice thought that there was something different about her eyes, something that could be curiosity but could almost be fear.

'I hear you've been having an exciting time, girls,' said Helena.

'Hardly exciting,' said Justice. 'Letitia has been kidnapped.'

It was the first time she had said the word aloud and she felt the reverberations spreading from their table until they reached every corner of the dining hall. Eva gasped and Helena clicked her tongue disapprovingly.

'You're exaggerating to make yourself important as usual, Justice.'

'Am I?'

'Yes, you are.' Helena's eyes narrowed. 'And, if you know anything about Letitia's disappearance, I strongly advise you to tell Miss de Vere. It's never a good idea to keep secrets.'

Helena stalked away, head held high. Justice watched her go, her usual feelings of irritation towards the head girl now combined with something more sinister. *It's never a good idea to keep secrets.* Could Helena possibly know about the note? Was this a sign that Justice *should* go to the headmistress? *No,* she told herself. Helena was simply doing what she did best: blaming Justice for everything. Justice had come across Helena on a few of her previous night-time adventures. She could only hope that the head girl wouldn't choose tonight to take a midnight stroll in the grounds.

This time it wasn't hard to stay awake. Justice had started to recite old murder trials, but other words and phrases kept whirling around her head:

Tower midnight tomorrow. Don't tell
Someone will pay for this
I Have taken Her
We promise to have fun
You're Veronica Burton's daughter, aren't you?

Sometimes you can see her walking through the grounds in
her white nightdress
The situation is desperate now. I'm scared of what he might
do
It's never a good idea to keep secrets.

Justice was ready by a quarter to midnight. The dormy was silent. Fear and stress were making the other girls sleep soundly. Justice put on her outdoor coat, which she'd hidden under her mattress, and held her shoes in her hand. Barefoot, she walked lightly to the door and opened it. Still no sound. At the end of the dormy she could see moonlight streaming in through the gap in the curtains. She remembered Letitia drawing back the curtains and saying 'full moon'. Was that only two nights ago? Well, the moon would still be almost full. Justice would be able to see whatever lay ahead of her in the grounds, even without the help of her trusty torch. She edged out of the door and started her progress along the corridor.

Miss de Vere had told her – rather pointedly – that the scullery door was now locked. Hutchins had a duplicate set of all the keys, but Justice had never given back the key she'd put in her pocket on the night of the midnight feast. At the foot of the maids' staircase, Justice put on her shoes and switched on her torch. She could hear the grandfather clock ticking from the great hall. Otherwise the house was sleeping. Justice swept her torch along the scullery passage, the light picking out the stone floor and the whitewashed walls, the bells for the servants. Justice crossed the scullery and inserted her key in the lock. The door opened easily.

Now she was outside in the grounds, the grass white with frost and the moon high over the trees. Justice ran through the kitchen gardens and, this time, took the path that led to the gymnasium and the Tower.

She had wondered if there would still be policemen in the grounds but she didn't see a soul, unless you counted a fox trotting towards the woods, who stopped and looked at her with utter disdain. She passed the covered swimming pool and now she could see the Tower with the moon directly above it, like an illustration in a book. From the house, she could hear a clock chiming midnight. *Better hurry*. Would there be someone waiting for her at the Tower? Would it be Letitia or the person who had kidnapped Letitia? For the first time, Justice realised how stupid she'd been. She'd left no note, so no one would know where she was. The Barnowls would wake up in the morning and realise that another of their number had mysteriously disappeared. Eva would almost certainly have hysterics.

Justice almost turned back but she was nearly at the Tower; her detective instincts were now stronger than her fears. She crept through the wood, trying not to tread on any frost-covered twigs. The heavy oak door of the Tower was shut. Justice stood, hidden by a pine that smelled of Christmas. An owl hooted overhead; otherwise, everything was silent. Then she saw it. A white envelope poking out from the foot of the door. Justice looked around. Was that a shadow moving quickly through the trees? Now she was sure that she could hear the crunch of footsteps.

Justice darted forward, grabbed the envelope and hared back towards the house. She was through the wood and heading towards the gymnasium. Then her foot caught on something and she was falling forward. Falling into nothingness.

CHAPTER 18

There was white all around her. Was she dead? Was this heaven? But then she heard a voice saying, 'I think she's coming round.' Miss de Vere. Justice was pretty sure that she wouldn't be meeting Miss de Vere in heaven.

Justice opened her eyes and saw Miss de Vere and Matron looking down at her. She closed her eyes again.

'Justice!' said Miss de Vere, more sharply this time.

'Where am I?' said Justice. 'Was I sleepwalking again?' This had worked once before, so she thought it was worth a try.

'You fell into the empty swimming pool,' said Miss de Vere. 'Ted the gardener found you. This was next to you.'

She held out the white envelope. Justice saw now that it had 'Lord and Lady Blackstock' written on it.

'I've telephoned Lord and Lady Blackstock,' said Miss de Vere. 'Now, why don't you tell me what you were doing in the grounds last night.'

Last night? Was it morning now? Justice knew that she was in the sick bay – she recognised the white walls now – but the sky outside was still dark.

'It's six a.m.,' said Matron. 'Ted found you when he came into work. You must have tripped and fallen. You were lucky not to be more badly hurt.'

Someone had once died after falling into the old swimming pool. Justice wondered if Matron had been told that story. How badly *was* she hurt? Her head ached but otherwise she felt fairly normal. Justice tried moving her hands and feet. Everything seemed to be working all right. She realised that she had several blankets on top of her, as well as her coat.

'You fell into the shallow end,' Matron was saying. 'The tarpaulin had come loose. Ted thinks a fox might have chewed through the fastenings. You didn't fall far but you hit your head quite badly and you were very cold. Ted had to carry you to the house. Miss de Vere has telephoned Dr Price.'

Miss de Vere had certainly been doing a lot of telephoning. Was it too much to hope that she'd go away now and ring someone else?

'I'm waiting, Justice,' said Miss de Vere.

Justice took a deep breath and told the headmistress about the message in *Murder in Milan* telling her to go to the Tower at midnight. She told her about seeing the envelope and running back to the house.

'I don't remember any more,' said Justice, trying to sound quavery. 'My head hurts a bit.'

'Honestly, Justice.' The headmistress sounded as if she was breathing hard. 'I despair of you. Why on earth didn't you bring the note to me? I would have told the police and perhaps we would have caught this person. We'd have Letitia back with us, back with her parents.'

'The note said "don't tell",' said Justice. This sounded pathetic when she said it out loud.

'And so you decided to confront the kidnapper on your own,' said Miss de Vere. 'Really, Justice, I'm at my wits' end with you. I've made allowance after allowance for you. I knew you'd never been to school before but I hoped that a few terms at Highbury House would teach you how to behave. But it seems as if we've had no influence at all. You still think that you can disobey the rules whenever you feel like it. I think it's time for us to part company. I've telephoned your father. I've asked him to take you away from the school.'

Another telephone call, thought Justice dully. One brief conversation to end her time at Highbury House.

After Miss de Vere had gone, Matron told Justice to try to get some sleep. Justice closed her eyes and was rather surprised to be woken ten minutes later by Matron and Dr Price. The doctor was a small, angry-looking man with a Welsh accent. He examined Justice, told her that she had concussion and needed to rest.

'The real danger is from the cold but you seem to have warmed up nicely. You're lucky not to have broken any bones.'

'I know,' said Justice.

She didn't feel lucky, and this must have shown in her voice. Dr Price suddenly sounded much kinder.

'Are you in trouble?' he said. 'Don't worry. We all got into trouble at school. It's not the end of the world.'

It's the end of my life at Highbury House, thought Justice. Suddenly she remembered crying in the barn and Ted saying, 'When things get to me, miss, I always tell myself: tomorrow will be better.' But tomorrow wouldn't be better. Tomorrow Letitia would still be missing and Justice would be back home, disgraced, expelled. Would she be allowed to say goodbye to Stella and Dorothy? She might never see them again. She realised that she was crying.

Dr Price patted her shoulder. 'Cheer up, now. At least you get a day off lessons, eh? Don't worry, Matron. I'll see myself out.'

'Try and rest now,' said Matron. She, too, sounded kind. 'It might all come right in the end.'

This time Justice couldn't sleep. She heard the thunder of footsteps when the girls went down to breakfast. She wanted to call out but they would never hear her. Would they be talking about her? The Barnowls must have noticed she was missing. Maybe Miss de Vere had already told them that she'd been expelled. Rose would be pleased. Or would she? It was hard to tell. Helena, on the other hand, would be delighted.

Matron brought her tea and toast and bustled about the room, tidying up and putting things in the wardrobe. Then she left Justice on her own. Justice was just drifting into an uneasy sleep when she heard a beloved and familiar voice outside.

'Is she in here? Thank you, Matron.'

'Dad!' Justice flung herself into her father's arms. Now she was really sobbing.

'I'm sorry,' she said. 'I'm sorry that I'm being expelled.'

'There, there,' said Dad, sounding comfortingly like his

usual self. 'Don't get upset, Justice. It's not good for you. Lie down again.'

'But I'm being expelled,' wailed Justice. Why didn't Dad understand?

'You're not being expelled,' said Dad, pushing her back on to the pillows. 'I've just seen Dolores— Miss de Vere, and she's decided to give you a second chance. She's still very angry, though, and I can't say I blame her. How could you put yourself in danger like that?'

Justice couldn't take it in. She wasn't being expelled. She could stay at Highbury House.

'I'm surprised to see you smiling,' said Dad. 'I thought you hated boarding school.'

'I do,' said Justice. 'Well, maybe I don't. I'm used to it, I suppose. And I've got friends here . . .'

'I know,' said Dad. 'I've just seen Stella. She sent her love and she asked me to give you this.' It was a Get Well card, drawn by Eva. It showed Justice riding a horse and carrying a shield that said 'Justice for all'. All the Barnowls had signed it.

Justice felt tears coming to her eyes again.

'You've got good friends here,' said Dad.

'I know,' said Justice, rubbing her eyes. She felt rather peaceful, the way you often do after a cry.

'Just try not to break so many rules in the future,' Dad

was saying. 'This is a serious business. It looks as if this Letitia has been kidnapped.'

'Yes, it does,' said Justice. 'Dad? When we first met Lord Blackstock, he seemed to know you. Why was that?'

'Asking questions already,' said Dad. 'You must be feeling better. I came across Lord Blackstock in court once. No' – he raised his hand to stop her speaking – 'he wasn't accused of murder. It was an embezzlement case. Someone was caught stealing from the Blackstock estate. Lord Blackstock is a very wealthy man. I'm afraid that's why someone has taken Letitia.'

'Have they asked for a ransom?' said Justice. 'Was that what was in the envelope I found by the Tower?'

Dad sighed. 'Yes, that's right. They've demanded five thousand pounds for the safe return of Letitia.'

'Five thousand pounds,' repeated Justice. 'That's such a lot of money. Are they going to pay?'

'Lord Blackstock wants to pay,' said Dad. 'But I think the police are trying to set up a trap.'

'I wish I could help.'

'Justice,' said Dad, sounding quite stern. 'I forbid you to get involved in this. Leave it to Miss de Vere and to the police. Do you understand?'

'Yes, Dad,' said Justice. Her dad patted her arm and told

her to look after herself. He had to get back to London because he was still in the middle of the trial. It was only when he got up to leave that Justice said, 'Dad? Why were you talking to Miss de Vere?'

'I beg your pardon?' Herbert stood in the doorway, his hat in his hand.

'I heard you in the North Turret talking to her. Right at the beginning of term. Was she using her radio?'

Herbert sat down on the bed. 'I always forget what a good detective you are, Justice. Dolores— Miss de Vere, has had a telephone line installed in the North Turret for . . . er . . . sensitive conversations.'

'What sensitive conversation were you having with her?' Justice was surprised to hear that she, in her turn, sounded rather fierce. Her dad must have heard it too because he said gently, 'It's nothing to worry about, Justice. Miss de Vere and I are old friends.'

'So what were you talking about?'

Dad sighed. 'Miss de Vere has money worries. It's hard running a school. A lot of the parents don't pay the fees on time. Some of them don't pay at all. Miss de Vere had to borrow money from a rich man to pay her mortgage on the buildings. Now she's worried that she won't be able to pay him back.'

'Who is this rich man?' But Justice already knew. It was Lord Blackstock.

Miss de Vere must have relented slightly because, after Meal, Stella was allowed to visit Justice in sick bay.

'Justice!' Stella rushed forward to hug her. 'I've been so worried. When I woke up and you weren't in your bed, I thought you'd been kidnapped. We all did. Then Matron came in and said that you'd tripped and fallen in the grounds. Why were you outside last night? Is it to do with Letitia?'

Once again, Justice told the story about the message in *Murder in Milan*. By the end, Stella had her hand over her mouth in horror.

'Justice! You could have been kidnapped yourself! Or killed! What did Miss de Vere say?'

'She said I was expelled.'

Stella gasped.

'But then she changed her mind. She came to see me this afternoon. She's taken the form captaincy away from me.'

'Oh, Justice.' There were actual tears in Stella's eyes. 'I'm so sorry.'

'It's all right.' If Justice had been told this news the day before she would have been distraught, but now it seemed like nothing compared to the threat of expulsion.

'How did you hurt your head?' asked Stella, eyes round with sympathy.

'I fell into the old swimming pool. So stupid of me. Apparently Ted the gardener found me and carried me back to the school. Helena will be very jealous.'

'She was asking questions about you at Meal.'

'Probably hoping that I'd been expelled. Anyway, we've got some more clues. The envelope that I found at the Tower had a ransom note in it. I wish I'd seen it. I wonder why it was sent here and not to Lord and Lady Blackstock? I wonder why the kidnapper wanted me to find it?'

'But you're not going to carry on investigating, are you?' said Stella. 'Not after what Miss de Vere said. And even your father told you not to.'

'Dad asked me if I understood and I said yes. I do understand. I won't put myself in danger again. But it doesn't stop me keeping my eyes and ears open. You never know, I might solve the mystery.'

'As long as you just sit and think,' said Stella, 'and don't go wandering around at night.'

This reminded Justice of Lady Blackstock talking about her mum's books. *I love the way Leslie Light solves the crimes just by sitting and thinking. So clever.* Was there something she was missing? Something to do with the Blackstocks?

Stella was asking about Matron. 'Was she nice to you? She seems kinder than the old matron.'

'Yes, she was nice, but she kept fussing around the room when I was trying to sleep.' Justice thought of Matron opening and shutting drawers and doors, moving between the medicine cabinet and the wardrobe . . .

'*Stella!*'

Stella jumped. 'What?'

'I've just remembered. I saw something in that wardrobe. I was half-unconscious but I know I saw it.'

'What did you see?'

Justice got up from the bed and went to the large wooden wardrobe in the corner of the room. She half expected it to be locked but it wasn't. Inside was a spare nurse's uniform and a billowing white dress, embroidered with tiny white flowers.

CHAPTER 19

'Justice!' Stella grabbed her arm. 'Is that the dress the ghost was wearing?'

'That was no ghost,' said Justice. Even so, they both jumped when the door creaked open.

'Can I come in?' said Dorothy's voice.

'Dorothy!' Justice pulled her into the room. 'I'm so glad to see you.'

'Are you all right?' said Dorothy. 'In the servants' hall they said you fell into the open swimming pool and broke your neck. I thought it wasn't true, though. Doctor Price looked quite cheerful when I saw him this morning.'

'I'm fine,' said Justice. 'I just hit my head.' She put her hand to her forehead and was interested to feel that there was now a lump there.

'What happened?' said Dorothy, sitting beside Justice and Stella on the bed. 'Mrs Hopkirk said that you saw Letitia's kidnappers.'

'I didn't,' said Justice. 'But I saw their ransom note.' She gave Dorothy a brief summary of last night's events and was relieved that this friend, at least, didn't scold her for being reckless.

'How thrilling,' said Dorothy. 'But you've no idea who's been leaving these messages? It must be someone who knows your mum's books quite well.'

'That's true,' said Justice. 'But there's more. Look in that wardrobe over there. Go on. It's open.'

Dorothy looked quizzical but she went to the wardrobe and opened the door.

'Oh, my goodness,' she said. 'Is that—?'

'I think it's the dress that the so-called ghost was wearing the night that Letitia was kidnapped,' said Justice. 'It got caught on a rose bush. Inspector Deacon showed me the fabric that had been torn off.'

'Has this dress got a rip in it?' said Dorothy.

'Good point,' said Justice. 'Let's look.'

Dorothy took the dress out of the cupboard. It was dark outside now and the white material glimmered and glittered in the gloom. Dorothy handled the satin gently, running it through her fingers.

'Here it is,' she said. 'It's been darned, but I can tell. Mum does mending sometimes. Here. Look.'

Justice looked and could just make out a crescent of tiny stitches. She would never have spotted it herself.

'Quick,' said Stella. 'Put the dress back. Matron could come in at any minute.'

'She won't. She's having her supper with the other teachers,' said Dorothy.

'In that case,' said Justice. 'Let's have a look around.'

Matron's room was next to sick bay but the door was firmly locked. There was a little bathroom but the only interesting thing in there was a bottle of hair dye called Joyous Jet. Five minutes later, the girls were back sitting on the bed.

'So what have we found out?' said Dorothy. She seemed very happy to be part of the investigations.

'That Matron isn't a natural blonde?' said Stella.

'Maybe not,' said Justice. 'But is she a kidnapper?'

'She can't be,' said Stella immediately.

Justice sighed. Despite everything they had been through, Stella could never seem to accept that staff members were capable of committing crimes.

'Either she is, or she knows who it is,' said Justice.

'Maybe they borrowed the dress without her knowing,' said Dorothy.

'That's true,' said Justice. She tried to sit and think, like Leslie Light. Should she go to Miss de Vere? But the headmistress would be furious that she was interfering in the case. Dad would be too. But, on the other hand, it *was* a clue.

'I need to telephone Inspector Deacon,' she said at last. 'He said I could contact him any time.'

'But where will you find a telephone?' said Stella. 'The only one in the school is in Miss de Vere's study.'

'There's one in the North Turret,' said Justice. 'Someone told me about it. I'll go there tonight.'

To their credit, neither Stella or Dorothy told her not to go.

When Matron came back, Justice was sitting up in bed trying to look innocent. Matron was carrying a mug on a tray. She put it down on the bedside table.

'Can I go back to the dormy?' said Justice.

Matron felt her forehead. 'You don't seem to have a temperature. Is that bump sore?'

'No. A bit.'

Matron handed her the mug. 'Drink this hot milk. It'll help you sleep. Then you can go back to your dormy.'

Justice loathed hot milk and this had a horrible skin on the top, but she snapped her insides shut and forced herself to gulp it down.

'Finished.'

'Very well, Justice. Go and join your friends. And try not to get in any more trouble.' Matron smiled.

Up until then, Justice had thought her a sympathetic person, softer somehow than some of the other teachers. But now she wondered if the warmth was false. Did the smile reach Matron's eyes? Or was she actually regarding Justice very intently, as if wondering how much she knew?

The Barnowls were all in the dormy. They stopped talking when Justice walked in.

'Justice!' Eva rushed over. 'Are you all right? We've been so worried.'

'Nora's form captain now,' said Rose. 'Have you heard?'

'Yes,' said Justice. 'Congratulations, Nora.'

'I'm sorry,' said Nora. 'I feel awful about it.'

'Don't worry,' said Justice. 'I was just relieved not to be expelled.'

That intrigued them, as she knew it would, and the girls gathered around her while she told the story for what felt like the hundredth time. Then there was the scramble to get washed and ready for bed before Matron came for her nightly inspection.

As soon as her head touched the pillow, Justice wanted to sleep. *You have to stay awake*, she told herself. *You have to telephone Inspector Deacon. Letitia's life might depend on it.*

But the next thing she knew, light was streaming in through the window and Rose was telling her to hurry up and use the bathroom before breakfast.

CHAPTER 20

Justice had lost count of the days and so was mildly surprised to discover that it was Saturday. Letitia had now been missing for four days, since Tuesday night. On Saturdays they had lessons as usual in the mornings but the afternoons were devoted to sport. Today there was going to be a lacrosse match which meant that Justice – as almost the only girl in her year not to be in the team – would get a few hours to herself.

'I'll try to get to the telephone in Miss de Vere's study,' she whispered to Stella, when they were lining up for breakfast.

'But how?' Stella whispered back.

'Miss de Vere will probably be watching the match. She might leave her room unlocked.'

'What happened last night? Why didn't you go to the North Turret?'

'I don't know. I just slept so deeply. Do you think Matron put something in my hot milk?'

'*Drugged you?* No, that can't be possible.'

They had to stop talking because they'd reached the front of the queue. Cook slopped porridge into their bowls and gave them her usual malevolent stare. She really did seem to hate young people, thought Justice. That must be why the food tasted the way it did.

The talk at breakfast was all about lacrosse. Justice tuned out and looked across the room. What were the other girls talking about? Letitia? Or had she already been forgotten? She saw Helena Bliss staring at her and went back to her cold porridge. Today, come what may, she would telephone Inspector Deacon.

In English they rehearsed the end-of-term pantomime. Justice always found this embarrassing because she and Rose had most of the lines. Also, in Justice's opinion, Rose overacted dreadfully.

'Oh, my dear brother, Hansel,' said Rose, batting her eyelashes, 'what are we going to do? We are lost in this horrible, dark wood.'

'Never fear, Gretel,' said Justice. 'I've been laying a trail of stones that will lead us back to our mother and father.'

'Oh, Hansel.' More eyelash stuff. 'You're so clever.'

'Very nice, Rose,' said Miss Crane, the English teacher. 'Justice, could you try to sound more protective of your little sister? Maybe put your arm around her? Remember, you're the big brave brother.'

Justice did not feel particularly big or brave but she put her arm around Rose (who flinched), and tried to put more feeling into her lines.

'Come, sister,' she said. 'Let us stop at this little house and get some rest before starting the journey home.'

'Oh, Hansel,' said Rose, wriggling free of Justice's arm. 'Do look! The roof is made of gingerbread and the door knocker is a peppermint.'

They had to stop there because Chona, who played the wicked witch, wasn't in their class. Justice was relieved. She'd had enough of being Rose's brave older brother and all the talk of sweets was making her hungry.

The lacrosse team had an early lunch so Justice ate on her own, watched by a group of first formers who seemed to expect her to sprout horns and a tail at any moment. As soon as she could, she escaped to the common room. On one side was the door to the courtyard; on the other, the windows opened on to the grounds. She could hear excited voices outside as the spectators made their way to the lacrosse pitch. Highbury House was playing a neighbouring school called Totteridge Towers. The second, third and fourth forms all had teams playing.

Would the Totteridge girls know about Letitia's disappearance? Would the teachers be warning them to stay together, to be careful in the dangerous grounds of Highbury House? And what was happening about the ransom note? Dad had said that Lord Blackstock wanted to pay but the police planned to set a trap. Oh, it was torture not knowing what was going on.

Justice waited for ten minutes, then she went to the door. The courtyard was empty, just autumn leaves blowing across from the trees outside. Justice crossed the courtyard and made her way along the kitchen corridor to the maids' staircase. On the first floor she paused, listening. Everything was silent. It seemed as if the whole school was out on the playing field. Justice could hear the clock ticking downstairs and the creak of the floorboards expanding. She froze when she heard Mrs Hopkirk, the housekeeper, talking to Cook on the floor below. But Cook was saying that she was going to lie down 'after making lunch for those varmints', and Mrs Hopkirk announced her intention of walking to the village.

Justice waited until their voices had died away and then she opened the little door that led to the spiral staircase that led to Miss de Vere's study. *Please God*, she prayed, *make it be open*.

But God wasn't listening. The door was locked.

Justice wasn't sure what to do next. Maybe she should go up to the North Turret to see if she could find the mysterious second telephone? That was risky, because the sixth formers had their common room in the attic and Justice was pretty sure that some of them would be in there. The sixth form wouldn't be bothered about a lower school match; they'd be snuggled up by the fire reading film magazines. Still, she had to try. But, as soon as she got to the attic stairs, she heard a most unwelcome voice.

'Justice? Is that you?'

Helena Bliss, coming down the stairs, dressed in her red winter coat.

There was no point trying to run away. Justice stood at the foot of the staircase waiting to see which rule Helena was going to accuse her of breaking. Helena had once given Justice an order mark for 'breathing too heavily', so there was bound to be something.

But instead Helena said something so amazing that, at first, Justice couldn't take it in.

'Justice. I need your help.'

CHAPTER 21

For a few seconds, Justice just stared at the head girl.

'Don't gape at me like that,' said Helena. That sounded more like the old Helena.

'Did you say you needed *my* help?'

'Yes. Come with me. It's not safe to talk here.'

Helena led the way downstairs until they came to an empty classroom on the first floor. There were Latin words written on the blackboard. *Amo. Amas. Amat. I love. You love. He, she or it loves.*

Helena looked around and seemed satisfied that they wouldn't be overheard. She sat on a desk. Justice did the same.

'It's about Ted,' said Helena.

'Ted the gardener?'

'Yes.' Helena was silent for a moment, fiddling with her charm bracelet. Then she said, 'I've been to see Ted a few times. He's got a cottage in the village and I chat to him in the garden. It's out of bounds but Miss de Vere mostly lets me do what I want as it's my last term.'

As far as Justice could see, Helena had always done exactly what she wanted. But she said nothing. She wanted to hear what Helena had to tell her.

'I went there yesterday,' said Helena. 'I was just sitting in the garden, waiting for Ted to come out, when I heard a voice. A girl's voice.'

'Just sitting in the garden.' Helena had made it sound as if Ted had invited her to visit but this seemed more as if she was lying in wait, like a cat with a mouse. Did Helena just sit there waiting for him to emerge? And . . . a girl's voice?

'At first I thought he was with a girlfriend,' said Helena, 'but I've been thinking . . . what if it was Letitia? What if Ted has kidnapped her?'

Justice wanted to say that this was ridiculous. Ted seemed nice. He'd comforted Justice when he'd found her crying in the barn, he'd rescued her last night. Last night . . .

'Ted was in the grounds last night,' said Justice. 'He found me when I fell in the empty swimming pool. The thing is, the kidnapper must have been in the grounds too, because they left a note at the Tower.'

'I know,' said Helena. 'I heard about that. It made me wonder all over again.'

'You should tell Miss de Vere,' said Justice. 'Or the police. That's what I was trying to do. To get to the telephone in the North Turret.'

'Why were you trying to telephone?'

Justice hesitated. Should she tell Helena about the dress? She still wasn't sure that she trusted the head girl.

'I thought I'd found a clue,' she said. 'I can't tell Miss de Vere because she told me not to get involved. I was almost expelled yesterday. But she'd listen to you.'

'Maybe.' Helena was still twisting her bracelet. 'It's just . . . I don't want people to know that I was . . . visiting Ted.'

'What does that matter?' said Justice. 'If we find Letitia.'

'Let's go and look now,' said Helena. 'That's why I wanted to find you. You know about all this detective stuff. I know you were involved the other time. You'll know what to do if Letitia is in Ted's cottage.'

'I'd call the police immediately,' said Justice. 'I've got Inspector Deacon's number.'

'That's the deal, then,' said Helena. 'If we think that

Letitia is there, we'll call the police. There's a telephone in the village pub. We'll go there.'

This sounded very daring. Women never went into pubs on their own. Justice wondered if the rumours about Helena visiting the pub with various boyfriends were actually true.

'Shall we go now?' said Helena. 'While everyone is at the match?'

'All right,' said Justice.

She'd known all along that she couldn't resist.

It felt very strange to be walking through the grounds with Helena, almost as if they were *friends*. True, Helena walked slightly in front of Justice and didn't address one word to her, but it still seemed odd. They walked past the lawn with the oak tree. Was it only last month that Mr Davenport had asked them to draw it? The smooth circle of lawn now looked shaggy and unkempt. The playing fields were on either side of them and Justice could hear shouts and applause from the lacrosse pitch. She hoped that the third years would win, even though Rose would be insufferable if she scored the winning goal, which she probably would. Helena stalked on ahead in her red jacket, her golden hair lifting in the wind. It was a cold afternoon and Justice wished that she'd brought her coat.

Ted's cottage was on the outskirts of the village, one of a row of three. It was really not that far from the school. Could Letitia really be here, so close to them all? Helena seemed to know her way well. She opened a gate and led Justice through a small garden, which looked as if it was usually full of vegetables. It was October now, though, and the earth was bare, apart from a few lettuces under a glass cover.

'Listen!' Helena hissed. 'Can you hear anything?'

Justice strained her ears but she could hear nothing except the noise of the wind. She even thought she could make out cries, very faint and far off, of 'Well played!'

Helena beckoned and they crept past some cucumber frames to the front of the little cottage. It was tiny really, just a door and one window on the ground floor and one window on the floor above. Justice thought of Hansel and Gretel. *Do look! The roof is made of gingerbread and the door knocker is a peppermint.*

'Justice!' Helena grabbed her arm.

Someone was coming out.

There was no time to run away. Justice and Helena just stood there as the door opened wider and a man appeared: hat, beard and a coat that looked like a cape.

'Mr Davenport!' gasped Justice.

'Justice. Eleanor. What are you doing here?'

'It's Helena.' Even now, the head girl sounded outraged that one of the teachers didn't know her name.

Something about the art teacher, maybe his steady gaze – not shocked but rather troubled – made Justice decide to trust him.

'We thought . . . we thought Letitia might be here . . .'

To Justice's astonishment Mr Davenport didn't laugh, or tell them not to be impertinent. He rubbed his beard and said, 'I thought the same thing but there's no one here. Friend Ted seems to have vanished. I did find this, though.'

He held out his hand. It was one of the bootlaces Letitia used to tie up her hair.

'That's Letitia's,' said Justice.

'I thought it was. We need to tell Miss de Vere. Come on, girls.'

Miss de Vere was at the match so Mr Davenport told them to wait outside the headmistress's office. Helena and Justice stood by the wall in silence. Justice thought that they were both stunned to be proved right. It looked as though Letitia *had* been in the gardener's cottage.

It didn't take long for Miss de Vere to join them. Justice could hear her footsteps – light but firm – running up the stairs. Miss de Vere appeared a few seconds ahead of

Mr Davenport. She unlocked her office, sat behind her desk, asked the girls a few questions and then telephoned Scotland Yard.

'Inspector Deacon, please.'

Justice couldn't help feeling slightly excited. She was there, at the centre of the action. Miss de Vere was talking to the inspector. Soon, he'd be back at Highbury House. Maybe he would want to interview her . . .

When she'd finished speaking and hung up the receiver, Miss de Vere looked at Justice.

'I thought I told you not to interfere,' she said, her eyes cold.

'Please, Miss de Vere,' said Helena. 'It was my fault. I asked Justice to go with me. I was scared to go on my own.'

Justice could hardly believe her ears. Helena Bliss coming to her defence! Helena actually admitting that she was in the wrong!

Miss de Vere looked rather shocked too. 'That was wrong of you, Helena,' she said, but her tone was milder. 'You should have come straight to me. However, we'll say no more about it. You may go, girls. Edward, can you wait a moment?'

Justice realised that Miss de Vere was talking to Mr Davenport. It was easy to forget that teachers had first names. 'Miss de Vere,' she said. 'There's one more thing.'

'Indeed?' Miss de Vere raised her eyebrows.

'There's a dress in Matron's wardrobe. I think it's the dress the ghost was wearing in the grounds the other night.'

Miss de Vere and Mr Davenport exchanged a look.

'How can you possibly know such a thing?' said Miss de Vere.

'I looked. When I was in sick bay.' Justice wasn't going to mention Dorothy.

'Of course you did. Very well, Justice. I will ask Matron about the dress. Dismissed.'

The girls clattered down the stone staircase. On the landing, Justice turned to Helena. 'Thank you for standing up for me in there.'

Helena shrugged. 'It was nothing.' She examined her nails for a second and then said, 'Justice, where do you think Ted's gone? Do you think he was the kidnapper?'

'If he's really vanished, it certainly looks suspicious,' said Justice.

'I can't believe it,' said Helena. Then she seemed to brighten. 'Mr Davenport's quite good-looking, isn't he?'

Justice despaired, she really did.

CHAPTER 21

It was agony waiting for the match to be over. Helena had stalked away without another word, so Justice was alone in the third-year common room until the door swung open and the room was full of what seemed like hundreds of girls, all talking at once.

'In the last few minutes . . .'

'. . . ball went to ground . . .'

'. . . definitely in the goal circle . . .'

'. . . and then Rose scored . . .'

'Rose was wonderful . . .'

'Rose . . .'

'Rose . . .'

Justice saw Stella and rushed over to her.

'Did you win?'

'Yes. Ten–seven. Rose scored a hat-trick.'

'That's great. Listen, I need to tell you something.'

She pushed Stella into the courtyard and told her about the afternoon's adventures. Stella seemed fixated on the fact that Helena had asked for Justice's help.

'I thought Helena hated you.'

'So did I.'

'Mind you,' said Stella. 'She was asking about you at Meal last night. And I saw her looking over at breakfast this morning.'

'So did I, but I just thought she was looking for a reason to tell me off. Anyway, we've made real progress. I can't wait for Inspector Deacon to get here.'

'A black car was pulling up at the main entrance when we got back from the match.'

'Really? Why didn't you say so?'

'I didn't think much about it.'

'The inspector must be here. I wonder when he'll send for me.'

But Justice had to wait all through Meal and an endless evening in the common room, listening to the wireless and to the girls talking about Rose's lacrosse prowess. She looked out of the window and saw torch lights. Were the police searching the grounds? Why weren't they talking to her? *She* was the one who had found all the clues. Justice banged her fists against the glass in frustration. Rose asked her if she was having a fit.

It wasn't until they trooped up to bed that Miss de Vere emerged from the door that led to her staircase.

'Justice. A word, please.'

The other girls looked at her curiously as they continued up the stairs. Miss de Vere led Justice into an alcove with the obligatory velvet curtains and gloomy oil painting.

'I thought you might be interested in knowing how the investigation is progressing,' said the headmistress.

'I am,' Justice assured her.

'This does not mean that I want you involved in any way, do you understand?'

'Yes, Miss de Vere.'

'The police have searched Ted's cottage and found some evidence of a girl's presence. They have also found a railway timetable.'

'So Ted might have taken Letitia away?'

Miss de Vere raised her eyebrows. 'Please don't interrupt, Justice.' Then, relenting slightly: 'It looks as if he may have taken her up north, to Scotland. I believe he has relatives there. I have also asked Matron about the dress. She tells me that it's her wedding dress, kept for sentimental reasons. She was married fairly recently. As far as I am concerned, that settles the matter.'

It didn't settle things for Justice. What about the tear that had been mended? But Miss de Vere was looking so forbidding that she didn't dare to interrupt again.

'Inspector Deacon may wish to speak to you,' Miss de Vere was saying. 'Until then, you are to stay with your dormy and on no account venture outside on your own. Is that clear?'

'Yes, Miss de Vere.'

Miss de Vere gave her one of her piercing looks before turning on her heel and heading back towards her office.

Justice stood still, thinking. Was the dress simply a wedding dress? Had Ted taken Letitia to Scotland? What was the evidence found in the cottage? Was it the bootlace or something more?

'Psst!' said a voice.

Justice jumped. The curtain twitched back to reveal Dorothy, feather duster in hand.

'I heard everything,' she said. 'Has Ted really kidnapped Letitia? I can't believe it. He always seemed so nice.'

'That's what Helena Bliss said,' Justice told her. She filled Dorothy in on the afternoon's adventures.

'So now you're friends with Helena,' said Dorothy. 'That's wonderful.'

'I doubt if we'll ever speak to each other again,' said Justice. She was fed up with people concentrating on Helena – in Justice's opinion, the least important person in the story.

'What about Matron?' said Dorothy. 'Do you think she's innocent?'

'I still think she's involved somehow. After all, you found that mend in the dress.'

'I suppose it could have got torn another way. There's a wedding photo in her room. I'll have a look at it when I light her fire tonight.'

'That would be great,' said Justice. 'I suppose I'd better go up to the dormy now.'

'Come to my room later,' said Dorothy. 'Then we can a proper detective chat.'

Whether it was because she hadn't drunk any of Matron's hot milk, or because her mind was buzzing with ideas and schemes, Justice had no problem staying awake. First she wrote in her journal.

The Disappearance of Letitia.

More clues

The white dress in Matron's wardrobe. Is this the dress that the 'ghost' was wearing? The material looks the same and there's a tear in it. If so, is Matron the kidnapper?

The hot milk. Was Matron trying to make me sleep heavily. Or to poison me?

The voice in Ted's cottage and the bootlace Mr D found. Is this proof that L was there? Miss de Vere mentioned other evidence. What could that have been?

Justice stopped writing. The other girls all seemed to be asleep. Eva was squeaking again. They were probably all exhausted from their exertions on the lacrosse pitch. Rose was almost certainly dreaming about her hat-trick.

Justice got out of bed and pulled on her dressing gown. She remembered the night that Letitia had followed her to Dorothy's room. Justice had been so angry. If Letitia ever reappeared, she would be nicer to her. After all, Justice realised suddenly, all Letitia had ever wanted was to be her friend.

Justice moved quickly along the corridor, trying to be as silent as a ghost. She could hear the wireless playing in Matron's room. Good, that would mean that her attention was occupied. Justice sprinted across the landing and took the steps to the attic two at a time.

Dorothy was waiting for her, still in her maid's uniform.

'I'm so glad you're here.' Dorothy pulled her into the room. 'Look what I've found. It's Matron's wedding photo. Not the one she keeps on her dressing table. This was in one of the drawers.'

Justice didn't say that Dorothy shouldn't be looking though Matron's belongings. She would have done the same. She took the framed photograph which showed a man and a woman smiling in front of a church. The bride was definitely wearing the same dress that was in the wardrobe. Then Justice looked again.

'The bridegroom. Surely that's . . .'

'Yes,' said Dorothy triumphantly. 'It's Ted. Matron is married to Ted.'

CHAPTER 23

On Sundays they had to walk to church. Justice found the services rather boring but she always enjoyed the walk and the chance to escape from the school grounds. Today, she made sure that she and Stella were at the back of the line and she whispered the news about Matron and Ted.

'I can't believe it,' said Stella. 'Matron is married to Ted! Why did she keep it a secret?'

'Maybe because they were planning to kidnap Letitia. Matron knew how rich Lord Blackstock was. He lent Miss de Vere money to keep the school open. That's probably why all the teachers were so soft on Letitia.'

'How do you know? About the money, I mean.'

'My dad told me.'

Miss Morris was at the front of the line with Sabre. She

turned round and shouted: 'Keep up, Justice and Stella. Don't fall behind.'

'Probably afraid that we'll be kidnapped too,' said Justice, as they increased their pace.

'No one would kidnap me,' said Stella. 'My parents are far too poor.'

There wasn't another chance to talk. They reached the church and filed into the front pews. Miss Morris tied Sabre up outside. Justice wished she could stay with him. She let her mind drift during the service as the vicar talked about forgiveness and Miss Evans played seemingly random chords on the organ. Had Ted and Matron kidnapped Letitia? It made sense in a way. Ted had been in the grounds on the night that Justice had gone to the Tower. Matron had said that he was on his way to work but she would say that, wouldn't she? Ted could have borrowed Matron's dress, to terrify the Barnowls on the night of the midnight feast so they would run away and leave Letitia to get kidnapped. He had blondish hair, Justice seemed to remember. So did Matron, of course. And it could just as easily have been Matron impersonating Grace Highbury . . .

'Let us pray,' intoned the vicar.

Please God, Justice prayed, *please let Letitia be all right. Please let us find her.*

Miss Evans launched into something like 'Thine Be the Glory'. Outside, Sabre howled. *Obviously a music critic*, thought Justice. Then, after a final blessing, the girls marched outside into the weak, winter sunshine.

Justice and Stella didn't talk much on the walk back to school. Justice was wondering if she should go to Miss de Vere. She'd be accused of interfering again, but surely it was worth it? But maybe Miss de Vere already knew that Matron was married to the gardener. Surely employers asked that sort of thing?

The crocodile of girls trudged along the road with the marshes on one side, the long grass whispering in the wind. Justice had often run this way with the cross-country team but it seemed longer when they were walking. It was colder too. The girls were just wearing their gabardine raincoats, which were no match for the icy air. Justice plunged her hands into her pockets and kept her head down. Eventually, they turned in at the school gates, the stone griffins looking as if they too were feeling the cold.

The girls started walking faster, looking forward to getting inside and drinking hot chocolate (a Sunday treat). Justice and Stella were left behind again. Justice looked at the path, half expecting to see Letitia-sized footprints, but there were just fallen leaves and the occasional acorn.

And . . . what was that? A seed? Some sort of pellet? Justice bent down.

'What is it?' said Stella, stamping her feet to keep them warm.

Justice held out her hand. In her head, she heard Letitia's voice, 'Keep your palm flat.' She smelled the stables and the horses. Heard the stamp of hooves and the jingle of bridles.

'It's a pony nut,' she said.

Pony nuts. I always carry some with me. Even in my dressing gown.

Then she heard her own voice, acting the part of Hansel.

Never fear, Gretel. I've been laying a trail of stones that will lead us back to our mother and father.

'Stella!' Justice grabbed her friend's arm. 'Letitia's left a trail for us!'

'What?'

'I think she's left a trail of pony nuts. We know Ted moved Letitia from the cottage – perhaps because he realised Helena had heard her voice. What if he's moved her here, into the house, right under all our noses? Let's see if we can find some more.'

It was Stella who found the next one, on the edge of the oak lawn. Justice found another by the steps to the main entrance.

'Did she come this way?' she said. 'That means she did come into the school.'

The other girls had all gone inside now. It was only a matter of time, though, before Miss Morris came looking for them. She'd been their form teacher last year so she knew Justice's tricks of old.

'Here's another,' said Stella. 'By the wall.'

'She went this way,' said Justice. 'Quick! Before Miss Morris comes out.'

They skirted around the side of the school. At first they thought they'd lost the trail but then Stella found another pony nut near the pig sties. One of the sows was snuffling hopefully at it from behind the bars of her gate. There was another on the path that led to the kitchen gardens. Then another in the flower bed, empty now apart from brownish stalks.

'It's lucky they haven't been eaten by foxes,' said Justice, remembering the fox who had supposedly chewed through the fastenings of the swimming pool cover.

'It means they haven't been here long,' said Stella. When had Ted moved Letitia? Was it only yesterday, before Justice and Helena had arrived at the cottage?

Justice wondered if the trail would lead to the Tower. Everything seemed to end up there, somehow. But then they saw another pellet on the path that led to the scullery entrance. And another on the step.

'She came back into the house,' said Justice. 'She came in through the kitchens. Just like we did on the night of the midnight feast.'

The back door was open. They could smell Sunday lunch (boiled cabbage and overcooked meat) and hear Cook complaining about something. Then a clatter of dishes and Ada, the scullery maid, apologising. There were no pony nuts in the kitchen corridor. Justice thought it was probably swept far too regularly. But, as they started up the maids' staircase, they found another pellet on the first landing.

'She came this way!'

First floor, second floor. They looked along the polished floorboards of the corridor and then, just when they were about to give up, Justice spotted a pony nut by the attic stairs. They ran up the narrow staircase and stopped at the top. They could hear dance music coming from the sixth-form common room. The only other rooms on this floor were Dorothy's bedroom and the art studio. At the end of the corridor, the door to the North Turret was firmly shut.

As they stood panting on the landing, the studio door opened and Mr Davenport emerged, paintbrush in hand.

'What are you girls doing here?'

'We followed a trail . . .' said Justice, suddenly feeling very stupid.

'We th-thought . . .' stammered Stella, standing on one leg. 'We thought that Letitia might be here.'

Once again, Mr Davenport didn't laugh and he didn't mention them being out of bounds. When they had finished their rather confused explanation, he said, 'Wait here. I'll get Miss de Vere.'

Miss de Vere appeared a few moments later. She looked tired and rather cross.

'I see you've been busy again, Justice.'

'We followed a trail of pony nuts,' said Justice, in a small voice.

'I see.'

They looked in every room, disturbing the sixth formers as they lounged around their common room, some still in their pyjamas. They looked in the studio and Dorothy's bedroom, even in the turret room. But there was no sign of Letitia.

'Perhaps some extra prep will take your mind off detective work,' said Miss de Vere.

Justice didn't really mind the extra history prep. It was quite soothing to write about Elizabeth I and forget kidnapping for a while. But later, when she was in bed, she found that she couldn't stop thinking about it. *Was* it Letitia who had left the pony nut trail? And, if so, was she hidden in the house somewhere?

Then, suddenly, she remembered a passage from her history prep. *'In 1585 Elizabeth's attitudes to Catholics changed. Catholics were banned from attending mass. Some Catholic families hid priests in so-called priests' holes but, if found, they could be sentenced to imprisonment or death . . .'*

And she remembered her first history lesson of the year with Miss Hunting.

'Miss Hunting, last year you said that there might be a priest's hole in Highbury House. A place where a Catholic priest might hide.'

'That's correct, Justice. I do believe that there's a priest's hole here . . .'

Miss Hunting had implied that the priest's hole was in the cellars, but what if it was at the opposite end of the house, in the attics? She thought of the top floor, under the eaves. Dorothy's bedroom was too bare for anything to be hidden. And as far as she could remember, the sixth-form common room had plain whitewashed walls, unlike the panelling in the studio.

The art studio.

Justice had a sudden memory of peeking at Mr Davenport's drawing of Irene. He had concentrated on the panelled wall behind her. Very elaborate panelling, as Justice remembered it.

Justice got up and pulled on her dressing gown. She took her torch from under her pillow and, as she had done many times before, she tiptoed across the room and along the dormitory corridor.

Justice tapped on Dorothy's door. 'It's me,' she hissed.

Dorothy appeared, in pyjamas, her mousy hair standing on end.

'Dorothy,' said Justice. 'Do you have the key for the art studio?'

'Yes,' replied Dorothy, rubbing her eyes. 'I was going to clean it tomorrow.'

'Can I have it?'

Dorothy went back into the room and emerged in her dressing gown, the key in her hand. 'I'm coming with you.'

The studio was at the opposite end of the corridor. Everything was silent, but Dorothy was the only person who slept in the attic. Or was she?

Justice opened the door. The room smelled of paint and turpentine. Dorothy switched on the light. The rows of chairs looked somehow sinister, as if they were waiting for something. Justice went to the teacher's easel and tried to work out where Irene had been sitting that day. Yes, she had had her head underneath that stag's head. And the panel below the stag had strange carvings on it. A pelican and a fish. Justice went closer.

'What are you doing?' hissed Dorothy.

'I think there's a priest's hole here.'

'A *what*?'

'A hiding place.'

Justice touched the fish. Was this an odd thing to find on a panel? The tail protruded from the woodwork. It was very lifelike, with tiny scales engraved in the wood. You could almost imagine it whisking through the water. Justice put her hand on the tail and pressed down. Instantly, the panel swung open, leaving a square black hole.

Dorothy gasped.

And a voice said, 'Justice? Is that you?'

CHAPTER 24

'Letitia!'

Justice shone her torch into the hole. Letitia was sitting crouched in the small space. When Justice held out her hand, Letitia grasped it and Justice pulled her into the room.

'Are you all right?' asked Justice.

'Yes.' Letitia straightened up. She was still in her pyjamas and dressing gown, which were now very dirty and mud-stained. Her face was dirty too, as if she'd been crying. But she was almost laughing now, holding on to Justice's arm. 'I thought you'd find me! Did you follow my trail of pony nuts?'

'Yes, but—'

'Letitia,' said Dorothy. 'Who kidnapped you?'

'It was Ted the gardener,' said Letitia. 'Wait till I tell you all about it.'

'Not now,' said Justice. 'We have to get Miss de Vere. And the police.'

'What's going on?' said a voice from the door. They turned around to see Matron standing there, serious and neat in her nurse's uniform.

'Matron!' Letitia ran forward. 'Justice found me! I was hidden behind the panel. And before that I was in Ted's cottage . . .'

'Letitia . . .' said Justice warningly.

But Matron already had her arm around Letitia. 'You poor thing. Let's get you down to sick bay and give you something to calm you down.' They moved towards the door.

'Stop!' shouted Justice. She rushed forward to grab Letitia's arm. 'Don't trust her! She's married to Ted.'

Letitia looked bemused. It was a lot to take in, thought Justice. Being captured, imprisoned and now released. No wonder Letitia suddenly looked as if she were unsteady on her feet. She swayed, clutching at Justice.

'She needs medical treatment.' Matron took her other arm.

'Help!' screamed Dorothy. Her voice echoed around the high-ceilinged room. They heard footsteps on the stairs and a man appeared in the doorway: Mr Davenport, wearing pyjamas, dressing gown and an old-fashioned nightcap on his head.

'Letitia!' he exclaimed. 'What are you doing here?'

'We found her in the priest's whatsit,' said Dorothy. 'And now Matron's trying to abduct her again. She's involved in it all. She's married to Ted.'

'Married to Ted?' said Mr Davenport. 'What are you talking about? We need to get Miss de Vere. Come with me, Letitia.'

Mr Davenport now came forward and took hold of Letitia's arm. Matron did not protest. She stepped back, looking slightly confused. Dorothy looked at Justice.

Justice jumped forward and pulled off Mr Davenport's nightcap.

He turned angrily. And Justice saw that, whilst Mr Davenport's beard was jet black, his hair was light brown. And she thought of her portrait of the art teacher, the way his hair seemed a different colour from his beard. She thought of Letitia wearing her fake Mr Davenport beard. And of the dye in Matron's bathroom. Joyous Jet. Dye to turn light hair jet black.

'There's no Ted,' said Justice. 'Mr Davenport is Ted. That's why you were coming out of Ted's cottage the other day,' she continued. 'You must have decided to move Letitia and put the blame on the non-existent Ted. You probably left the railway timetable for the police to find, trying to convince them that Letitia was in Scotland.'

'Rubbish,' said Mr Davenport. And, for the first time, Justice heard a Scots lilt in his voice.

'Run!' said Justice, grabbing Letitia's arm. Mr Davenport darted forward but Dorothy tripped him up. Then all three girls were running for the door.

'Edward!' shouted Matron. 'Stop them!'

Ted is short for Edward, thought Justice, even as she hurtled down the corridor with her friends. Why hadn't she thought of that?

They were at the top of the stairs but Mr Davenport was right behind them. He grabbed the cord of Letitia's dressing gown and pulled her back.

'Let her go!' Justice tugged at Letitia's arm but the teacher was far stronger. He took hold of Letitia and looked as if he was about to drag her back into the studio when, suddenly, he stopped. A figure appeared in front of them. Someone in a white dress with long, blonde hair.

'Grace Highbury,' breathed Dorothy.

The figure raised its hand and pointed at Mr Davenport. He stepped backwards. Justice grabbed Letitia's arm and, pushing past the ghostly figure, galloped down the stairs. Dorothy was close behind her.

They stopped on the landing, panting. *What should we do?* thought Justice frantically. *Should we go to Miss de Vere's room or head for the front door?* But then Justice heard voices on the floor below.

'Come on!' They ran down the next flight of stairs.

And cannoned straight into Inspector Deacon and his men.

'Mr Davenport,' panted Justice. 'He kidnapped Letitia. He's up there.' She pointed towards the stairs.

'Look after them,' said Deacon to one of the two officers. 'Come with me,' he said to the other. And they sprinted upstairs.

The girls stared at each other. Letitia was still looking confused. Justice was shaking.

'Did you see the ghost?' Dorothy panted. 'The ghost of Grace Highbury?'

'That wasn't a ghost,' said Justice. 'That was Helena Bliss.'

'Did you see how scared he was?' said a new voice. 'I can't stand cowardly men.'

Helena was smiling at them. In her billowing, white

181

nightdress, with her hair loose, she really did look a bit like someone from the past. Or an angel.

'I was in the common room,' she said. 'I often go up there when I can't sleep. I heard voices and worked out what was happening. I thought I'd try and give old Davenport a scare.'

'You succeeded,' said Justice. 'He believes in ghosts. He told us that during our first lesson. You saved us.'

'Girls!' Miss de Vere appeared on the landing, wearing a rather grand Japanese kimono. 'What on earth is happening? I came out of my room to find Inspector Deacon arresting Matron and Mr Davenport. Oh, Letitia, my dear! Are you all right? Are you hurt?' She put her arms around Letitia, who wriggled free.

'Justice found me,' said Letitia. 'You should be thanking Justice.'

Miss de Vere looked at Justice over Letitia's head. She was smiling. 'Thank you, Justice,' she said.

CHAPTER 25

The next few hours were very exciting. Miss de Vere ushered them into the staff room and actually brought them mugs of tea on a tray. Had she made the tea herself? Dorothy's eyes were wide as she accepted her cup. Then Lord and Lady Blackstock burst into the room. Lady Blackstock flung herself on Letitia, sobbing and laughing at the same time. Lord Blackstock blew his nose loudly and looked as if he was trying not to cry. Then Lady Blackstock let Letitia go and swept Justice into her arms. 'Miss de Vere told us that you were the one who actually found Letitia. How can we ever thank you?'

'It was nothing.' Justice felt pleased and embarrassed at the same time. She was glad that she'd seen the pony nuts and then remembered the priest's hole, but she couldn't help thinking that she should have solved the mystery earlier. Why didn't she stop to consider how odd it was that blonde Matron should possess black hair dye? And she'd caught Mr Davenport actually coming out of Ted's cottage – why hadn't she noticed the likeness? Maybe it was the beard, which must have been false. Maybe it was because, Justice suddenly realised, that she had never really looked properly at Ted – all because of that silly rule about pupils not mixing with so-called servants. But Helena, who *had* looked at Ted, had also thought that Mr Davenport was handsome. Justice should have been suspicious then.

Lady Blackstock hugged Dorothy and Helena too. Then Dorothy asked the question on everyone's mind: 'Lady Blackstock, why did Mr Davenport kidnap Letitia?'

Lady Blackstock sat on the sofa, still holding Letitia's hand. Lord Blackstock stood in the doorway, as if afraid to let his guard down.

'It goes back a long way,' she said. 'When Letitia was little we commissioned Edward Davenport to paint her portrait. He was quite an up-and-coming painter then. We don't know much about art and maybe it was a good likeness, but we thought it was too unflattering and so we sacked him. He must have harboured a grudge all these years.'

'Letitia told me that story,' said Justice, 'when I came to your house on the half holiday.'

'So all this trouble could have been avoided,' said Letitia, 'if you'd only admitted that I was an ugly child.'

'You weren't ugly,' said Lady Blackstock, indignant even now. 'Edward Davenport was just one of those modern painters who don't want things to be pretty.'

Justice thought of Mr Davenport saying to her, 'You're not a flatterer, Justice.' Maybe that had been a compliment, after all? He'd been commenting on the portrait Justice had drawn of Letitia, the one showing the bootlace tying back her hair. Mr Davenport must have pretended to find the bootlace in Ted's cottage, she realised, knowing she would recognise it. Mr Davenport had also told her to 'look harder'. She should have taken his advice.

'There was a silly article in a magazine about Letitia coming to Highbury House,' Lady Blackstock was saying. 'That must have given Davenport the idea. He got his wife to apply for the job of Matron too. She was a nurse, apparently.'

The school really should take more care when appointing matrons, thought Justice. *That's three in two years.* She realised that she was very tired and her thoughts were becoming rather incoherent.

'I saw the article,' she said. 'Rose – one of the other girls – showed it to me.'

'Typical Rose,' said Letitia. 'I can't wait to see the Barnowls again.'

'You're coming home with us,' said Lord Blackstock, speaking for the first time. 'And you're not coming back to this school.'

'Oh no, Daddy,' said Letitia. 'I love it here. I want to play lacrosse and see the Christmas pantomime. And I'd miss Justice and Stella. And Dorothy. Even Rose.'

'We'd miss you,' said Justice, realising that this was true.

'And think of the tricks we can play,' said Letitia.

Miss de Vere was standing by the window and Justice thought that she heard her groan.

They were all interviewed individually by Inspector Deacon.

'Good work, Justice,' said the inspector. 'Though you should have come to me as soon as you thought of the priest's hole. We were still stationed in the grounds.'

'Was that why you got here so quickly? I didn't think of telling anyone. I wanted to find out for myself.'

'How did you know where to find the secret panel?'

Justice told the inspector about Mr Davenport's drawing of Irene and how he had concentrated on the panelling and not on his subject.

'I should have guessed then,' she said.

'It was a good thought about the panel,' said Inspector Deacon. 'Miss de Vere was telling me that a fish is often a symbol of Christianity. Maybe that's why the priest's hole had a fish carved on it.'

'I think Miss Hunting said something about that in history. I should have listened more carefully.'

Deacon's lips twitched. 'Perhaps that's one of the lessons to take from this. Good detectives listen. And they're not afraid to ask for help, to be part of a team. You can't always do everything yourself.'

'I had Dorothy,' said Justice. 'And Stella. And Helena,' she added, as an afterthought.

'Was she the girl who pretended to be a ghost? Apparently she gave Davenport quite a fright. Even though he'd had the idea of dressing his wife up as a ghost on the night of your midnight picnic.'

'Was that Matron? I thought it was Ted at first.'

'Yes, she must have had quite a rush to get back into the house, change out of the white dress and take charge of the search for Letitia. No wonder the dress got torn.'

'What will happen to Mr Davenport now? And Matron?'

'They'll be charged with kidnapping,' said the inspector. 'And I hope they go to prison for a long time. Unless they get a good defence lawyer, like your father.'

Justice thought this must be a joke. 'Why did they send notes torn from my mother's books? And why did they send that note to me? About meeting at the Tower?' she said. 'That made it all seem very personal.'

'I think they sent the note to you because Davenport guessed you would investigate without informing the authorities,' said Inspector Deacon. 'It seems the other teachers were talking about your, er . . . independent nature.'

Justice thought that 'independent nature' was probably code for 'always breaking rules'.

'Davenport knew how much Lady Blackstock liked Veronica Burton's crime novels,' said Deacon. 'He must have seen her reading them when he was working at Blackstock Hall. I think he liked the idea of sending ransom notes from her favourite author.'

Justice shuddered. She hated to think of her mum's books being used in this way. Mum would have hated it too. She didn't even like it when people turned down pages to mark their place.

'Why did Mr Davenport pretend to be a gardener?' she said. 'Didn't that make things more complicated?'

'That was quite clever,' said the inspector. 'It meant he had a cottage, for one thing, as it came with the job. Quite daring to keep Letitia there, in the village, under all our noses. And it meant that, if things became tricky, he could shift the blame on to this mysterious Ted. We found a handkerchief in the cottage embroidered with the initials LB, plus the timetable open at trains to Inverness. It was all too obvious, really. We should have seen that something was wrong.'

'Mr Davenport liked experimenting with reality,' said Justice. 'He said so in our lessons.' She felt quite sad, remembering that she'd rather liked the eccentric art teacher. She also suddenly felt very tired.

Inspector Deacon saw her trying to suppress a yawn. 'Try and get some sleep now,' he said. 'It's nearly morning.'

But, as Justice walked slowly towards her dormy, she saw something that made her forget all thoughts of sleep: her dad, walking across the great hall, accompanied by Miss de Vere.

'Dad!' Justice bounded down the stairs.

Her dad caught her up in a hug. 'Justice! I might have guessed that you'd be involved in this. I knew as soon as Do— Miss de Vere telephoned me.'

'Well, it's all turned out for the best,' said Justice. Miss de Vere made a noise that might have been a laugh – or another groan.

'I do wish you could have one term without getting

yourself into danger,' said Dad, but he squeezed her shoulder while he said it.

'Why don't you two go into my sitting room and chat,' said Miss de Vere. 'I'll ask Cook to make you some breakfast. I ought to get the teachers together and tell them the news. It's nearly seven o'clock. The girls will be getting up soon. You can be excused lessons this morning, Justice.'

'Thank you,' said Justice. She'd forgotten her tiredness and now felt as though she were fizzing with excitement.

Miss de Vere's sitting room was by the main entrance; it was where she interviewed prospective parents, and it was full of trophies and flattering watercolours of the school. Justice and her dad sat in the window seat as the dawn light streamed in and Justice told him the whole story: about Letitia, the midnight feast, the white dress, the voice in the cottage, the trail of pony nuts, the priest's hole.

'My goodness, Justice,' said Dad, when she had finished. 'That's quite a story. Maybe you should be a writer one day.'

'I want to be a detective,' said Justice. 'Remember?'

'How could I forget?' said Dad. There was a slight pause and then he said, 'Justice?' All of a sudden, he seemed slightly nervous, fiddling with the tassel on the curtains. 'I've got something to ask you. I think now might be a good time.'

'What is it?' said Justice, but her heart was sinking. *He's going to marry Miss de Vere*, she thought. *I'm going to have to call her Mother. I can't bear it.*

'It's about Dorothy,' said Dad.

'Dorothy?' Justice felt her spirits slowly rising.

'She's such a bright girl,' said Dad. 'It seems wrong that she's a maid here and not a pupil. Especially as she's been such a good friend to you. Do you think her parents would be offended if I offered to pay the fees to send Dorothy here? Dolores has said she'd be happy to accept her as a pupil.'

'I think they'd be delighted,' said Justice. Her spirits were now positively soaring. Next term, Dorothy would be here as a pupil. Justice, Stella and Dorothy could all be school friends together. And Letitia too, she realised. Letitia was part of the gang now. She was even prepared to forgive her father that accidental 'Dolores'.

'As long as you don't go around looking for mysteries,' said Dad, with a slight smile.

'We won't,' said Justice. 'Surely there can't be any more mysteries left to solve.'

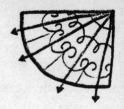

Acknowledgements

Justice is inspired by my mum, Sheila de Rosa, who was at boarding school in the 1930s. My mother had been brought up by her actor father and had never been to school before. She found it a bewildering place at first but, like Justice, she made lifelong friends amongst her classmates. Unlike Justice, she didn't get to solve any murders.

This book was written during the lockdown for the 2020-21 pandemic, which made me sympathise with the isolation of Highbury House. If my books have cheered anyone up during this strange time, then I'm very happy. I'm so grateful for the support of my publishers and my wonderful agent, Rebecca Carter. Thanks to everyone at Hachette Children's for working so hard on my behalf under very difficult circumstances. Special thanks to Sarah Lambert, Rachel Boden and Dominic Kingston. Thanks to Alison Padley for the beautiful cover design and to Nan Lawson for the brilliant illustration of Justice. Thanks also to my teacher sister, Giulia de Rosa, for her advice on art lessons.

This is a book about friendship, so it's dedicated to my grown-up children, Juliet and Alex Maxted, and their childhood friend, Monique Dingelstad. JAM forever.

Elly Griffiths 2021

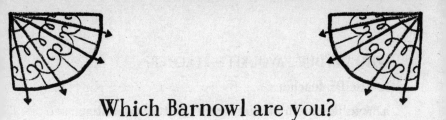

Which Barnowl are you?

WE ARE INVITED TO A BALL. WHAT DO YOU WEAR?

a. Tiara and ballgown

b. A nice dress, not too plain and not too showy

c. Party dress and newly mended glasses

d. Something dark so that you can sneak away without being seen. Low-heeled shoes for ease of escape. Bag for torch and pen knife

e. You're not sure what a ball is but think it sounds super fun

IT'S SPORTS DAY. WHAT IS YOUR BIGGEST FEAR?

a. That you won't have a bag big enough for all your trophies

b. That you'll show yourself up in some way

c. That your glasses will break

d. That you'll have to do something that requires catching or throwing

e. Sports Day is super fun. Why be worried about anything?

WHO IS YOUR FAVOURITE TEACHER?

a. The PE teacher
b. You like them all but haven't got a favourite
c. The English teacher because you like making up stories
d. You're not that keen on any of them
e. They're all SUPER

YOU GET AN ANONYMOUS MESSAGE TELLING YOU TO MEET THE SENDER IN THE HAUNTED TOWER AT MIDNIGHT. WHAT DO YOU DO?

a. Stay in bed. I need my beauty sleep
b. I'd be worried and tell a friend or a teacher
c. You think it will make a great story to tell people late at night
d. Go, of course
e. Scream! It sounds very scary

YOU THINK THE MAIDS ARE ...

a. There to do the dirty work for us
b. Very hard-working
c. Nice but I don't really know them
d. Valuable sources of information and possible friends
e. Super

WHAT SORT OF BOOKS DO YOU LIKE TO READ?

a. Romances
b. Non-fiction
c. Ghost stories
d. Detective stories
e. You're not that keen on reading

WHEN YOU GROW UP YOU WANT TO BE . . .

a. A debutante, going to balls and wearing lovely clothes
b. A doctor or a nurse
c. A teacher
d. A detective
e. Older

TURN THE PAGE TO FIND OUT YOUR RESULTS

Mostly A〔...〕ll and the Qu〔...〕they?

Mostly **Bs**. You are Stella. You just want a quiet life, to fade into the background and not be noticed. When faced with real danger, though, you can be brave and determined. Remember, there are worse things than standing out from the crowd.

Mostly **Cs**. You are Nora. You love telling stories and having fun. You're a great person to be around but be careful that you know the difference between real life and fiction. Oh, and watch those glasses . . .

Mostly **Ds**. You are Justice. You are brave, resourceful and obsessed with detective stories. Remember, though, you do need your friends sometimes and even the teachers aren't all bad. Also, midnight meetings can be dangerous.

Mostly **Es**. You are Eva. Your world is super. It's a nice place to be.